The phone on the
it took her a few
sound was.

Her heart was still pounding when she p
the receiver. "Hello?"

The voice on the other end was just a whisper.
"Hi, Babes. I'm back."

Sarah. L.

Point Horror

THE BABY-SITTER II

R. L. Stine

Hippo Books
Scholastic Children's Books
London

Scholastic Children's Book's
Scholastic Publications Ltd,
7-9 Pratt Street, London NW1 0AE, UK

Scholastic Inc.,
730 Broadway, New York, NY 10003, USA

Scholastic Canada Ltd,
123 Newkirk Road, Richmond Hill,
Ontario Canada, L4C 3G5

Ashton Scholastic Pty Ltd,
P O Box 579, Gosford, New South Wales,
Australia

Ashton Scholastic Ltd,
Private Bag 1, Penrose, Auckland,
New Zealand

First published in the US by Scholastic Inc., 1991
First published in the UK by Scholastic Publications Ltd, 1992

Copyright © R. L. Stine, 1991

ISBN 0 590 55062 4

10 9 8 7 6

THE BABY-SITTER II

Chapter 1

"I — I killed him," Jenny said, shifting uncomfortably on the couch.

"I can still hear his scream. So loud at first and then fading to . . . nothing. No matter how I try to look at what happened, I just can't get it out of my mind that I killed him."

She twisted a strand of her dark hair as she talked. Her eyes, so round and black, stared at the cracks in the wall beside her. She licked her lips, a nervous habit she just couldn't stop.

"I'm sorry," she said, taking another strand of hair and twisting it between her slender fingers. "You asked me to begin at the beginning, and I skipped to the end. It's just . . . so hard."

She took a deep breath and began again. "It was last fall, just a few weeks after school began. I go to Harrison. I'm a junior this year. I guess you already knew that." She let go of her hair and let her arm drop down, clasping her hands tightly in her lap.

"Well, I took this baby-sitting job. Twice a week with this adorable little boy named Donny. Donny Hagen. Donny had the most amazing white-blond hair you ever saw. He was so cute, and the two of us just hit it off right away.

"The Hagens lived in this creepy old house on the other side of town. It used to take me over half an hour to get there on the bus." Jenny paused. "I guess that isn't a very important detail. But sometimes I think about all those long bus rides, that nearly empty bus bumping across town in the dark, taking me to — to that frightening old house.

"Well, anyway, after I'd been baby-sitting for Donny for a short while, I started getting these really scary phone calls. I'd pick up the phone and hear this ugly whisper. And always the same words. *'Hi, Babes. Are you all alone? Don't worry, company's coming.'* "

Jenny shuddered. As she said the words, she heard the whispering voice once again in her ear. And felt the fear all over again.

"There had been all these attacks on baby-sitters all over town," she continued. "I kept hearing about them on the news. And here I was, all alone in this frightening old house on the other side of town. I had this new boyfriend. I guess you'd call him a boyfriend. We really hadn't gone out all that much. He was new at Harrison. His name was — is — Chuck. Chuck Quinn."

Jenny's features tightened into a frown. "I'm not

seeing Chuck anymore. He's — he's a real joker. You know, a class clown type. He's very funny, actually. But after . . . after what happened . . . I don't know. I guess I didn't feel much like laughing and joking all the time. So I told Chuck I didn't want to see him anymore. He was really upset. He got very angry. He has an angry, moody side, too, and — Oh. Sorry. I'm getting away from my story."

Her hands felt cold and clammy. She wiped them on her jeans. "I started to let Chuck come to the Hagens' house when I was baby-sitting there. I — I just felt safer when he was there. I mean, because of the scary phone calls. But then I started getting the calls at my own home. Always the same. '*Hi, Babes. Company's coming.*' It was so frightening.

"I started thinking maybe it was Chuck who was making the calls. I guess I was just freaked or something. But I didn't know Chuck that well. And he was a joker, always clowning around and playing practical jokes.

"I was so scared. I wanted to quit my baby-sitting job. But Mom persuaded me to stay. We really needed the money, see. Mom is a legal secretary. She doesn't make a very big salary. The Hagens were paying me five dollars an hour, and with Christmas coming up . . .

"So I stayed. And then one night I found the newspaper clippings up in Mr. Hagen's closet. They were all clippings about children who had died because of baby-sitters' carelessness. And clippings about the attacks on baby-sitters that had been happening all over town. And the baby-sitters' names were all circled in red!

"It was Mr. Hagen! He was the one, the one attacking the baby-sitters. Donny had had a sister. And the sister had died. And Mr. Hagen blamed the baby-sitter. I guess it destroyed his mind or something, made him crack up. And now he was out to get back at all baby-sitters.

"He — he was the one making the calls. He was the one — This is all so terrible. As I'm telling it to you, I'm seeing it all again." Jenny was clasping her hands together so tightly, it hurt. Suddenly realizing it, she let go and forced her hands down to her sides.

She waited awhile, waited for her heart to stop pounding. She took the glass from the table beside her and sipped some water. Then she took a deep breath and in a low, steady voice, resumed her story.

"Mr. Hagen came up behind me in his bedroom. He saw me reading his newspaper clippings. He knew that I knew. He — he said he was driving me home. But he didn't.

"It was very late. There were no other cars on the road. He drove to the old rock quarry. You know the one? About ten miles north of town?

"He pulled me out of the car and he hit me. *'This is what you deserve,'* he kept saying. *'This is what you deserve.'*

"He backed me up right to the edge of the quarry.

It was so dark. I was standing right on the edge, nothing but air behind me. It was such a nightmare. The headlights from his car were shining in my eyes. I was blind. But I knew if I took one more step back, I'd go over to the bottom of the quarry.

"And then he pushed me. I mean, he rushed at me. He meant to push me. But somehow I — I dodged away from him. And he went flying over the edge.

"I didn't see him. I only heard him. That scream. That horrified scream. I heard the scream all the way down. Then I heard the cracking sound his body made when it hit the rocks below."

Jenny paused, trying to catch her breath. "I still hear that sound. *Crack*. Like an egg breaking."

She was playing with her hair again, nervously braiding a strand of dark brown hair, still staring at the wall, but not seeing it, not seeing anything.

"Of course, I realize it wasn't my fault," she continued. "I mean, he was crazy. He was trying to kill me. I know that. I mean, I can tell myself that over and over. But I still have this . . . knowledge, this awful knowledge that I killed him, that I'm responsible for Mr. Hagen's death. That Donny doesn't have a father because . . . because . . ."

Her mouth felt as dry as cotton. She stopped to take another sip of water. The water was warm and tasted of minerals. She made a face, but took a long drink.

"When Mr. Hagen fell over the quarry edge, it was all over. The nightmare, I mean. He was dead.

No more attacks on baby-sitters. No more phone calls or threats. Donny and his mother moved away. I don't know where.

"I was safe, but it wouldn't go away. I mean, I tried to force it all out of my mind. But then the dreams started. The nightmares. Just about every night.

"They're so real, so vivid. I see them in color. I'm sure of it. And I remember them when I wake up in the morning. Every detail.

"In most of them, I see Mr. Hagen. I see him crawling up to the top of the rock quarry. His face is all twisted, all distorted, and he's covered with blood. In the dreams, I'm standing there watching him as he pulls himself up to the top. Then he starts to stagger toward me, like Frankenstein, only covered with blood, his clothes all torn. Sometimes his skin is all torn, too, and chunks of it are falling off his body. Sometimes he has a skull instead of a head, a bleeding skull.

"And I — I just stand there. I want to run away from him — but I can't. I'm paralyzed or something. And he comes closer and closer until . . . I wake up screaming."

Breathing hard, Jenny stared up at the tiled ceiling.

"I think we'd better stop there," Dr. Schindler said softly. "This session is almost up. We'd better save your dreams for next time."

He reached across his cluttered desk and clicked

off the tape recorder. Narrowing his green eyes in concentration, he popped the cassette from the machine and began to label it with his pen.

Dr. Schindler doesn't really look like a shrink, Jenny thought, turning her gaze on him. For one thing, he is too handsome. And too tanned. With his wavy, coppery hair, those blond eyebrows and startling green eyes, she imagined him as an actor or maybe a model.

And he looks too young to be a shrink, Jenny thought. Shouldn't he have a beard or something? Or wear thick, rimless eyeglasses? Or smoke a pipe?

He didn't look the part, but he had the diplomas to prove that he was the real thing. They were carefully lined up in rows on the wall behind his enormous mahogany desk.

"Next time — " he started to say, flipping through his appointment book.

"But what about my problem right now?" Jenny interrupted. She turned and pulled herself to a sitting position on the couch, dropping her feet to the floor. "You know. About the baby-sitting job."

The question seemed to catch him off guard.

He's forgotten everything I said at the beginning of the hour, Jenny thought, groaning to herself. No *wonder* he has to tape everything!

"Well, Jenny . . ." His eyebrows lowered, and his face assumed a more serious expression. "How do *you* feel about it? What do *you* think you should do about the job?"

Jenny sighed.

Was he just going to ask questions? Wasn't he going to *help* her?

"I don't know," she said, biting her lower lip. "Normally, I guess I'd have a real summer job now. But I was so upset, and so tired from never being able to sleep much, I just didn't think I could manage a full-time job."

She looked to him to reply, but he just stared back at her with those sparkling green eyes, his face completely expressionless.

"I need money for school in the fall," Jenny continued uncertainly. "And the Wexners seem like really nice people. They only live a few blocks from my home. And their son, Eli, is ten, so he probably won't be that much trouble."

"How often do they want you to baby-sit for Eli?" Dr. Schindler asked, fingering his silver-and-jade desk clock.

"Two days a week and two nights," Jenny told him. "It isn't too bad. And I really need the money. But — "

He stared at her, waiting for her to finish her sentence.

" — I'm really frightened."

"Frightened of — ?" he asked, leaning forward.

Jenny thought for a while. "I don't know," she replied. "Just frightened."

"Frightened that Mr. Hagen will come back?"

"No, of course not," she said quickly, feeling her face flush. "I know that's stupid. I don't know.

Should I take the job? I really should — shouldn't I?"

She expected him to react, but his face remained expressionless. "I hate to sound like a psychiatrist," he said softly, "but what do you *want* to do?"

"I want for it all to have never happened," Jenny said with more emotion than she had planned.

"That would be good," Dr. Schindler said, finally smiling. "But we can't go back in time. We can only go forward." He glanced at his desk clock.

"I — I think I should take the job," Jenny said, suddenly surprising herself by making a decision. "Yes. I do. I think I should take it. There's no real reason not to. And I really need the money. And maybe — maybe it'll help me get over all the fear. You know, like getting back on a horse after you've fallen off."

"You've made a decision," Dr. Schindler said. He seemed pleased by it. Or was Jenny just guessing about his reaction?

"Yes. I guess I have," Jenny said, tossing her shoulder-length hair back, smoothing it with one hand. "My problem is that I have this wild imagination. My mom — I mean, everyone — they're always telling me that my imagination runs away with me and — "

Dr. Schindler startled her by standing up.

He's so tall, Jenny thought. He's too tall to be a shrink!

"I'm sorry," he said, his eyes on the clock. He straightened his navy-blue necktie. "Perhaps we can talk about your imagination next week. I'll also want to hear how you're doing with your new job."

"Yes. Okay," Jenny said, feeling foolish. Her time was up, and here she was dithering on about her wild imagination.

Well, he doesn't have to be *such* a clock-watcher, does he? she asked herself. Is keeping to his schedule all he cares about?

"Would you like me to prescribe some sleeping pills?" Dr. Schindler asked, walking her to the door.

"Will they stop the bad dreams?" Jenny asked hopefully.

"I'm afraid not," he said without smiling, one large hand gently on the shoulder of her T-shirt.

"Well, then, I — I don't think so," Jenny said.

"Okay. But feel free to call me anytime if you'd like a prescription," he said. "Please see Miss Gurney on the way out."

As Jenny pulled open the door, revealing Miss Gurney, the receptionist, seated at the desk in the tiny waiting room, Dr. Schindler quickly removed his hand from her shoulder.

Jenny started to say good-bye, but he had already returned to his desk. She crossed the small room with its four brown leather chairs and stepped up to Miss Gurney's low desk in front of a wall of gray filing cabinets.

Miss Gurney was a plump, middle-aged woman, with gray-streaked black hair tied tightly behind her head in a bun. She was dressed in a gray skirt and white high-necked blouse, very conservative-looking except for her eyeglasses, which had bright red plastic frames dotted with rhinestones. She finished writing a long entry in a logbook of some sort, then looked up at Jenny.

"What a pretty T-shirt," she said in a surprisingly husky voice, looking Jenny up and down through the bizarre eyeglasses. "What do you call the way the colors all run together?"

"It's . . . uh . . . tie-dyed," Jenny told her, looking down at her T-shirt to remind herself what she was wearing. Her mind was still swirling from all that she had just relived in Dr. Schindler's office.

"Very pretty," Miss Gurney muttered, searching her desk for something. She found the pad she was looking for and wrote something on it, scribbling quickly in jagged, bold letters.

"This is just a reminder of your next session," she said. She tore off the note and started to hand it to Jenny but then sneezed loudly.

"*Gesundheit*," Jenny said.

"Lots of germs around here," Miss Gurney said, reaching into her desk drawer for a tissue. She handed Jenny the note.

"See you next week," Jenny said.

Clutching the note in her hand, she stepped out of the office, down the hall, and out the street door. She had expected to see bright sunshine. It was four in the afternoon. But the sky was evening dark. Puddles on the sidewalk indicated that it had rained while Jenny was in the doctor's office.

I wish I had driven here, Jenny thought, looking

up at the dark sky. Too bad Mom needed the car. It's going to start raining again any second. "Oh, well," she said aloud.

She turned and, chilled by the cool, wet air, began walking quickly down Wooster Hill. Dr. Schindler's office was located in a low office building at the top of the hill, surrounded by other office buildings and a few old residence hotels. The bus stop was at the bottom of the hill, four blocks down.

It began to drizzle, a cold drizzle for June. Being careful not to step into the deeper puddles, Jenny hurried down the hill.

The sky turned even darker. It was as black as night now. A cold wind seemed to follow her down the hill. Her sneakers splashed against the wet concrete sidewalk.

"Where *is* everyone?" she asked herself, looking around at the deserted street. "Guess everyone else has the good sense to stay in out of this cold rain."

She was in the middle of the third block, shivering from the cold, her hair wet, her T-shirt soaked through, when she heard the footsteps behind her.

Suddenly frightened, she turned back to see who it was.

No one there.

Strange.

She started walking down the hill again, taking longer strides.

Come on, Jenny. Don't start thinking things. Don't let your imagination start running away with you.

The rain came down harder.

She heard the footsteps again. They were hurrying, too, keeping pace with her.

A familiar fear gripped her chest.

I'm being followed, she realized.

Chapter 2

Without looking back, Jenny started to run.

"Hey — " a voice called angrily.

Whoever it was started to run, too.

The steady rain continued to fall, whipped by sudden, cold gusts of wind. The sidewalk dipped steeply, following the hill down to the bottom. Jenny's sneakers slid and slipped as she ran, jumping over puddles now.

A car turned up the hill from Oakland Avenue, its headlights on despite the early hour. The double lights caught Jenny, as if in a spotlight, and she shielded her eyes from the shock of the brightness.

And a hand grabbed her shoulder roughly.

She opened her mouth to scream, but no sound came out.

"Jenny — what's the matter?"

She spun out of the grasp, turned to face him, breathing hard. "Chuck!"

"Hey — why'd you run? Didn't you hear me calling you?" His expression was serious, concerned. He didn't have his usual, goofy Huck Finn grin. His curly blond hair was matted down on his head from the rain. Water ran down his freckled cheeks.

He was wearing a faded Bart Simpson T-shirt over jean cutoffs. His white Nikes were mud-stained and soaked.

"Chuck — what are you doing here?"

"Getting wet," he said. He never could resist making a joke.

"You — you really scared me," Jenny said angrily, her heart still pounding.

"I didn't mean to," he said. "Why'd you run like that?"

"I — uh . . . I thought you were someone else," she said, thinking hard to come up with an answer.

Why *had* she run like that?

It seemed pretty silly now.

And not silly. So many things frightened her now.

So many things reminded her of . . . other things.

"I *am* someone else," Chuck cracked. "That's why I was running. I was running from myself."

"Well, maybe you should keep on running," Jenny said coldly. She hadn't meant it to come out as harsh as it did.

Chuck gave her his hurt-little-boy expression. The dimple in his right cheek appeared, the dimple she used to be so crazy about.

Now she didn't feel anything.

He's so big, she realized. He's built like a wrestler. Did I ever notice how wide he is, how powerful he looks?

"Chuck, it's raining. I've got to get to the bus," she said impatiently.

"Your mom said I'd find you up here on Wooster Hill," he said, ignoring her impatience. And then he added meaningfully, "Your mom still likes me."

"Then why don't you go pester *her*?" Jenny snapped. She turned and crossed Oakland Avenue against the light. He hurried to keep up with her.

"Aw, come on, Jen — "

She kept walking, taking long strides. The bus stop was on the next corner. The street sparkled from the rain, all reds and purples.

Suddenly nothing looked real. The colors were all wrong. The sky was an eerie chartreuse. The street was a glowing purple. Everything seemed to be so wet, so shiny.

I'm walking in a dream, Jenny thought.

Chuck grabbed her arm again, gentler this time, bringing her back to reality.

She turned around, not quite sure why she felt as angry as she did. "Chuck — what do you want?" she cried, pronouncing each word slowly and distinctly, her voice hard and shrill.

"I just wanted to talk with you," he said, his eyes searching her face for some warmth. "I don't think we ever really talked after . . . " His voice trailed off.

"We talked and talked and talked," Jenny said

wearily. Half a block to go to the bus stop. The hill began to level off as it met Hunter Street. Beside her just beyond the sidewalk, rainwater poured down the curb, a steady downhill river. "I don't want to talk anymore, Chuck. I said everything I had to say. I don't want you following me anymore. I don't want you waiting for me, jumping out at me wherever I go."

The words seemed to pour out of her like the water rushing down the hill. She suddenly felt flooded with emotion, angry and sad at the same time.

"But, Jenny," Chuck said, refusing to let go of her arm. "I don't want to lose you."

Having said this, he let go of her and looked away.

He can't stand being this open, this vulnerable, Jenny thought. He makes jokes all the time, usually to cover up his true feelings. But here he is, letting me know how he really feels.

If only I had some feeling for him.

She stared at his face, so open, so fair and blue-eyed . . . so hurt.

She didn't want to hurt him. She felt a sudden pang, a sudden urge to say, "Okay, Chuck. Let's go talk. Let's go back to the way things were." But she knew that wasn't her true feeling. She knew she never could do that.

"I'm not the same person," she said flatly, wiping rainwater off her forehead with her hand.

"But, Jenny — " he pleaded.

"So much happened to me, Chuck. I'm just not the same person. It — it's not your fault. Really. It's all me. I know that. It's all my fault. But you've just got to accept it."

"I *can't* accept it!" he shouted.

His sudden anger startled her. She stepped back, into a deep, cold puddle. The water went over her sneaker, covered her white sock.

"I *won't* accept it!" he shouted.

Jenny tried to concentrate on him, tried to figure out what to say to him to make him realize once and for all that it was over between them. But the shimmering colors distracted her. The oddness of it all. The green sky that didn't look like afternoon or evening. The sparkling, slick streets. The glowing patches of blue grass beyond the sidewalk.

The two white circles of light that approached so quickly.

It was all out of focus now, all shimmering together.

And it took Jenny so long to realize that the two approaching lights, so white now, so bright, so close, were actually the twin headlights of the cross-town bus she'd been waiting for. It took her so long to make them seem real, she almost missed the bus.

But just before the driver gave up and reached to push the button to close the double doors, she leaped onto the step and pulled herself inside.

She could hear Chuck yelling angrily behind her, pleading with her to stay.

And as the doors closed with a soft *whoosh* and the bus strained away from the curb, its windshield wipers scraping across the rain-dotted glass, arcing to a steady, clicking rhythm, Jenny heard him threatening her and cursing.

Poor Chuck.

But she was being pulled away from him now, pulled away from his angry words, pulled as if in a dream, away, away, away.

I'm free, she thought, seeing Chuck grow smaller and smaller in the rear window of the bus. I'm free. . . .

"Hey — it's not free!"

The husky voice brought Jenny back to earth. "What?"

"The bus. It's not free," the driver barked. "You gonna pay?"

"Oh. Right. Sorry." Jenny searched her pockets for change.

I shouldn't have come here, Jenny told herself.

The sky was flat and starless. No moon. No clouds. The blackness was solid and deep.

I shouldn't have come here.

She stood on the hard ground, staring into the darkness, staring ahead to the bottomless pit that stood only a few feet in front of her, stretching out in both directions.

The rock quarry.

What brought her back here, back to the scene of all the horror?

What forces drove her to face it again? What did she hope to see *this* time?

Jenny, Jenny, said a voice inside her, you can't lose memories by chasing after them.

What a mysterious thing to say.

The darkness turned even darker, but she knew the treacherous hole was there. She knew she was standing near the edge, so near the edge she could almost *feel* the emptiness, almost *feel* the sheer drop of it.

I shouldn't have come here.

You can't lose memories by chasing after them.

What did it mean?

She had no time to figure it out.

Even in the darkness she could see the two hands shoot up on the top of the quarry edge. Even in the darkness she could see them grasp onto the rock.

Two hands from the pit. Two hands from down below.

Spattered with blood, they dug into the hard rock.

The man's head appeared next.

The hands pushed. The arms strained. The head seemed to rise up, like a pulpy, bloodstained moon. Like a dark-eyed, lopsided moon rising over a canyon.

"Mr. Hagen — no!"

He pulled himself up out of the hole and onto his knees. Part of the flesh of his face had been torn away, revealing curved bone under his cheeks. The rest of his flesh hung loosely about his fixed grin.

His eyes never left hers.

"Mr. Hagen — no!"

He laughed. The sound was nothing but wind, dry, dry wind. The sound of ashes.

He staggered toward her, his arms outstretched, bone protruding from the elbow of one arm.

"Mr. Hagen — it wasn't my fault!"

Even though her voice was coming from her own mouth, it sounded far away.

She tried to run. Her legs wouldn't move.

She couldn't even turn away from him. Couldn't even *look* away!

"Mr. Hagen — please!"

And she started to scream.

She opened her mouth, her eyes wide open, and screamed.

"Jenny — please! Jenny, Jenny!"

He was holding her. He had his broken arm around her. He brought his flesh-torn face close —

No!

"Jenny! Jenny — wake up!"

It was her mother who was holding on so tightly.

The dream, the horror of the dream, faded slowly.

"Mom — ?"

"Jenny. Jenny, wake up. You were dreaming again."

"What? I — "

"It was just a dream, Jenny. Another nightmare," Mrs. Jeffers whispered.

The room came into focus. The blue lamp on the

dresser. The curtains fluttering softly at her window. Her mother. Her mother looking so much older all of a sudden. Her mother looking so worried, so . . . frightened.

"I'm sorry, Mom," Jenny said, her voice tiny, still filled with sleep. "It was the same dream. I had it again."

"Jenny, Jenny," her mother whispered soothingly, her arms still tightly around Jenny's shoulders.

"It — it was so real," Jenny said.

"But it wasn't real," Mrs. Jeffers told her.

"It seemed as if I were really there. Standing there again."

"Jenny, Jenny," her mother repeated, "it wasn't real. Believe me, child — nothing like that will ever happen to you again."

Chapter 3

"Well, here goes."

Jenny stood at the foot of the gravel driveway, looking up the gently sloping lawn to the Wexners' house. It was a two-story, gray-shingled house, not very large, sort of a box without any style. A red-and-white boy's BMX bike stood leaning against the front stoop. The hedges that ran along the house from the stoop to the far side were neatly trimmed, and the grass looked as if it had been mowed with great care.

Her sneakers crunching up the gravel drive, Jenny felt a little bit less nervous. At least it's not a run-down old mansion like the Hagens' house, she told herself. The Hagens' house, she recalled with a shudder, looked like the setting for a horror movie. The Wexners' house, on the other hand, looked well cared for and inviting, Jenny thought.

From the drive, Jenny could see around to the backyard, which was also neatly mowed and dotted with tall evergreens. The sun was setting behind the trees, the sky a beautiful rosy gray.

Jenny climbed the three steps onto the stoop. She raised her hand to knock on the screen door, and a man appeared in the doorway.

"Oh, hi," he said, holding open the door. "I saw you coming up the drive. Did you walk here?"

"Yes," Jenny said, stepping into the house. "It's only two blocks from my house."

"Oh. Right. I think you told us that." He motioned for her to go into the living room, which was small but nicely furnished with a white leather couch and matching armchair around a glass-and-chrome coffee table. Three watercolor paintings of different-colored orchids were hung stairstep-fashion on the wall behind the white couch.

"I like the paintings," Jenny said.

"Oh, really?" Mr. Wexner seemed pleased. "Rena painted those. My wife. She's really quite talented. I keep after her to paint more, but she hasn't had the time."

He was a short, slightly built man, about thirty-four or thirty-five, Jenny guessed. His narrow, pleasant face was topped with thinning, light-brown hair that he wore combed straight back and as neatly trimmed as his front lawn. He was wearing a navy-blue, button-down sportshirt and neatly pressed chinos.

"Rena and I won't be out very late," he told Jenny, motioning for her to have a seat in the armchair. "We're just visiting friends."

"Where's Eli?" Jenny asked, looking out the front

window at a rabbit hopping near the stoop.

"Good question," Mr. Wexner said, smiling. "My guess is he's up in his room, building something or other. Eli, as you will quickly find out, is quite mechanical." He chuckled. "You will quickly find it out," he added, "because Eli will tell you what a mechanical genius he is. I'm afraid he's not too modest."

"Most ten-year-olds aren't," Jenny said, laughing.

"I wish Eli acted more like other ten-year-olds," Mr. Wexner said, his smile fading, his face filling with concern. "Oh, well. Back in a minute." He turned and hurried up the stairway across from the front door.

What did he mean by that? Jenny wondered.

She walked to the window and looked for the rabbit, but it had disappeared. A bookcase under the window contained three shelves of mysteries. She read the titles for a while, feeling nervous, wishing Mr. and Mrs. Wexner would leave so she could play with Eli or just relax.

"Hi, Jenny. Sorry to rush out without a chance to talk. I've written down the number where we can be reached on this pad." Mrs. Wexner, standing at the foot of the stairs, spoke rapidly in a soft whisper of a voice that barely carried across the living room.

She was a small, thin woman, shorter than Jenny, with blonde hair cut boyishly short, dramatic dark eyes, and three diamond studs in her left ear. She was wearing a pale blue, long-sleeved T-shirt over white tennis shorts, and sandals.

"Hi, Mrs. Wexner," Jenny said, stepping away from the bookcase.

"Please — call me Rena. Eli is upstairs in his room. Why don't you go up and say hi? He's expecting you."

"Okay — " Jenny started.

But Mrs. Wexner just kept right on talking. "Don't let him walk all over you, if you know what I mean. Sometimes you've got to be firm with Eli. But not *too* firm, if you know what I mean. He's very emotional. I mean — well, you'll see. He's so smart, you see. Sometimes we forget he's only ten, and — "

"Come on, Rena," Mr. Wexner called from the kitchen. "You'll scare Jenny away before she even starts!"

"Okay. Sorry," Mrs. Wexner said, her whispery voice making her sound like a little girl. "Sometimes I talk too much. But there are worse crimes, right?"

Jenny laughed. She didn't know how else to react. Mrs. Wexner seemed a bit surprised by her laughter. She picked up her bag, quickly fingered through it, then closed it, and hurried out toward the kitchen. "See you later, Jenny. Help yourself to anything," she called.

Jenny heard the kitchen screen door slam. A few seconds later, she heard a car start up. Jenny watched from the window as the Wexners' car, a blue Volvo station wagon, backed down the drive.

"Guess it's time to go meet Eli," she said aloud. As she climbed the stairs, she thought about Mrs. Wexner's words of warning. She seemed so nervous, Jenny thought. Why did she feel she had to warn me to be careful with Eli?

Is he some kind of monster or something?

Jenny's imagination immediately took over. She pictured a monster waiting for her at the top of the stairs, a short, hunched creature with bulging red eyes and an open, drooling mouth, giggling hideously to himself, waiting to pounce on her the second she came into view.

Stop it, Jenny, she scolded herself. He's probably just a little high-strung, she decided, reaching the top of the stairs. A narrow hall led to two bedrooms and a bathroom.

The door at the end of the hall proved to be Eli's room. Jenny stopped in the open doorway and peered into the room. Eli was seated at a long white counter that ran the length of the back wall. The counter was filled with all kinds of electronic equipment and tools. An M.C. Escher poster was the only artwork on the walls, a confusing abstract of tangled, interwoven shapes that seemed to double back on themselves endlessly.

Eli had his back to the door. He was typing rapidly on a computer keyboard, his face and body outlined in the amber glow of the monitor.

"Hi," Jenny called from the doorway.

He continued to type.

"Hello!" Jenny called, nearly shouting.

He typed a little longer, then spun around on his desk chair. "Hi," he said without smiling.

Jenny saw that he had a narrow, intense face like his father's topped with thick blond hair, which obviously hadn't been brushed that day. He had his mother's dark eyes, which were even more startling on him since his skin was so fair and the rest of his features were so pale.

He was wearing a "Turtle Power" T-shirt over green spandex bicycle shorts.

"I'm Jenny," Jenny said, venturing a few steps into the room.

"I know," Eli said, scratching one ear. "You're Jenny Jeffers. You live two blocks away on Sycamore. You go to Harrison High. You're going to baby-sit me two days and two nights a week."

"Hey — you're right," Jenny said. "I'm impressed."

He shrugged. "I don't need a baby-sitter," he told her, his face remaining expressionless, not unfriendly, not friendly.

"Maybe I do," Jenny joked.

"I built this computer," he said, ignoring her joke.

"You did? You built it? I really *am* impressed," Jenny exclaimed, moving closer to take a better look.

"From a kit," Eli said. "But I modified it. I put in a graphics card and extra memory."

"Wow," Jenny said, leaning over him to stare at the monitor screen.

"You know anything about computers?" Eli asked, sounding doubtful before Jenny even answered.

"A little. Enough to do my homework on."

He smiled for the first time. He doesn't look so grown-up and serious when he smiles, Jenny thought. Such a sweet smile.

"I really don't need a baby-sitter," he said, turning serious again. "You could go home right now, and I'd be perfectly fine."

Jenny couldn't help it. She felt a little hurt by his repeating this. "Would you *like* me to leave?" she asked.

He turned back to his computer. "I'm a mechanical genius, you see. At least that's what the testing people said. I took all these tests at this place downtown, and they said I was a mechanical genius. Know what my IQ is?"

"No. What?" Jenny asked, a little appalled by the boy's boasting.

"It's over 180. That's really high. And it'll probably go higher when I get older and know how to take tests better."

"Wow," Jenny repeated, not sure whether she should be encouraging him or lecturing him on why he should be more modest.

"What's *your* IQ?" he asked.

"I don't know," Jenny replied.

"No. Really," he said, reaching out and pulling her arm. His hand was so small, it startled Jenny. How did such little hands build this big computer?

"Tell me your IQ," he said, tugging her arm.

"I really don't know," Jenny insisted. "I don't think I've ever taken an IQ test."

"Why? Because you're too dumb?" He burst out laughing, a goofy, high-pitched laugh.

"That's not nice," Jenny said, unable to suppress a giggle. "I'm not dumb."

"Then why wouldn't they let you take an IQ test?" he asked, still holding onto her arm.

Is he being friendly? Jenny wondered.

Why is he holding onto me so tightly?

"I don't know. Let's change the subject," Jenny said impatiently. "Tell me about your computer. What do you do with it?"

"You wouldn't understand," he said, sighing.

"Why wouldn't I?"

"Because you're not a mechanical genius like me."

"That's not a nice thing to say, Eli."

Oh, brother, Jenny thought. Here I am with this kid for five minutes, and I'm already making with the lectures.

"I'll show you something else I built," he said, his large, dark eyes glowing in the amber monitor light. He held a finger up to his mouth. "*Ssshhh.*"

"Is it a secret?" Jenny asked, whispering.

"It's a secret from my parents," Eli said, pulling a cardboard carton out from its hiding spot beneath the counter.

"Maybe you shouldn't show it to me if it's a secret from them," Jenny suggested.

"It's okay. You're only the baby-sitter," he said.

I think he *meant* that to be cruel, Jenny realized.

I think maybe he's testing me, seeing how far he can go, how mean he can be. He's too smart not to know that he was insulting me. Or is he? He's only ten, after all.

Eli is definitely going to be a challenge, Jenny thought.

"See?" Eli asked, pulling a metal-and-wire contraption out of the carton.

"Wow," Jenny said, trying hard to figure out what it was.

He handed it to her. "It's a phone. Rena and Michael don't want me to have one."

"Rena and Michael?" Jenny asked, a little surprised.

"You know. My parents," he said impatiently. He took the homemade phone back and deposited it carefully in the carton. "They don't want me to have a phone. They're afraid I'll get spoiled."

"So you built your own?"

He nodded. "It really works. I tried it. There's a phone jack right under the counter there. See it?" He bent down to point it out to her.

"Who do you call with your secret phone?" Jenny asked.

He shrugged. "No one really. I mean . . . I don't have too many friends." His face remained expressionless as he said this.

Jenny felt uncomfortable with Eli's sudden openness. He was such a strange combination. One minute he was insulting her, telling her she was only the baby-sitter and he really didn't need her. The next moment he was holding onto her arm and confiding in her what had to be a painful secret.

"Do you *try* to make friends?" she asked.

"Friends are stupid," he said.

"What?"

"They're stupid. The kids at school. They're dweebs. Stupid dweebs."

Jenny didn't know how to respond to this. She didn't want to get into a heavy-duty discussion with the kid about the value of friendship. But she knew it wasn't right that he thought all the other kids were too stupid to be his friends.

"I'll show you my real friends," he said, pulling her by the arm.

"Your real friends? Eli — where are you taking me? Don't pull so hard!" He was surprisingly strong for such a skinny little kid.

"I just want to show you this," he said. "Close your eyes a minute."

Jenny obediently closed her eyes. When she opened them, Eli was holding a shoe box in front of her face. "What's in the shoe box?"

"Go ahead," he urged. "Reach your hand in."

"What?"

"It's okay, Jenny. I promise. Slide back the lid and put your hand in."

"No, I won't," Jenny insisted warily. "No way."

"Come on — I promise," he said. He looked upset, hurt that Jenny wasn't trusting him. "I promise. Please. Stick your hand in."

"Well. Okay. If you promise it's okay," Jenny said reluctantly.

He probably has a turtle in there, she thought. Or maybe a hamster or a guinea pig.

I don't want him to think I'm a dweeb, too.

She slid back the lid a few inches and plunged her hand into the box.

And then she opened her mouth wide and began to scream.

Chapter 4

"It was a tarantula," Jenny said, her voice trembling, just thinking about it. "Do you believe it? The kid put a tarantula in the box. He has three of them. They're his pets."

She stopped to scratch her arm. She suddenly felt itchy all over.

Dr. Schindler leaned forward at his desk, rolling a silver letter opener in his hand. "So what did you do?" he asked, his first words since Jenny had begun describing her first evening of baby-sitting for the Wexners.

"I — I screamed and dropped the box," Jenny said, picturing the big, hairy tarantula as she spoke. "The thing fell out of the box and started to run right toward me."

Dr. Schindler's face remained expressionless. He continued to twirl the letter opener.

"I dodged out of its way," Jenny continued. "I *hate* spiders. I've always hated spiders. But Eli, he thought it was hilarious. He was in hysterics. He laughed until tears rolled down his cheeks. I — I wanted to kill him."

"Not really," Dr. Schindler said quietly. He looked over at the tape recorder, checking to make sure the tape hadn't run out.

"Not really," Jenny agreed. "But it was such a mean trick. I mean, making me reach into that box. And then he thought it was so hilarious that he had frightened me, that his trick had worked.

"The look on Eli's face, it was . . . evil. That's the only way to describe it — evil. He just laughed and laughed."

"Then what happened?" Dr. Schindler asked, glancing at his clock.

"Eli put on a glove and picked up the tarantula, and carried it back to the glass case he keeps them in. He never even apologized. I told him that was a horrible trick to play on someone, and all he said was, 'Tarantula bites can't kill a person.' "

"He's ten, right?" the psychiatrist asked, writing a quick note on his desk pad.

"Yeah. But this wasn't like a ten-year-old's prank," Jenny insisted, suddenly feeling defensive. "He — he enjoyed it too much."

"What do you mean, Jenny?"

"I mean . . . he thought it was so funny that I got so frightened. I just had the feeling that he wanted to hurt me."

"Are you sure you're not reading too much into this?" Dr. Schindler asked.

"I don't think so," Jenny said. "I really don't."

"Well, what happened next? After he put the tarantula back in its cage?"

"I forced myself to calm down. But I was still very upset, and I told Eli how angry I was. I told him he should never play a mean trick like that again."

"Did he take you seriously?"

"I really don't know," Jenny replied, thoughtfully. "After I scolded him, he got real sullen. He turned away from me and went back to his computer. He wouldn't talk to me the rest of the night."

"Not at all?"

"Not at all," Jenny said, shaking her head. "I went downstairs and watched TV. I didn't see him the rest of the night. He even put himself to bed. I couldn't believe it."

"How do you know he put himself to bed?"

"I went upstairs to check on him about ten-thirty, and he was sound asleep, all tucked in his bed. It was so weird. I mean, I was angry at him. I don't think he had a right to be angry at *me*."

Dr. Schindler smiled for the first time in the session. "I don't think we should talk about *rights* when it comes to a ten-year-old."

Jenny frowned. "When his parents came home, I told them what had happened. They just looked at each other, like, 'Oh, brother, here we go again.'"

"What did they say to you?"

"Rena, Eli's mother, all she said was that I should try not to get Eli angry. She said once he gets angry, it's hard to win him back. They weren't apologetic or anything. And they didn't say anything about punishing Eli for what he did to me.

"They were only worried that maybe I got Eli mad at me. That's all they cared about. I got the feeling that Eli has had a *lot* of baby-sitters. He's so smart, but he seems to be real difficult."

"Do you think you can handle him?" Dr. Schindler asked.

Jenny shrugged. "I hope so. The Wexners are paying me five dollars an hour. I really would like to keep this job."

"Have you had any more nightmares?" Dr. Schindler asked. But then he looked at his clock. "Oh. Sorry. We'll have to talk about that next session." He clicked off the tape recorder and stood up.

Jenny stood up, too, feeling awkward. She never knew what to say after he turned off the tape recorder.

"Eli sounds like an interesting kid," Dr. Schindler said, raking his hand back through his coppery hair and then stretching. "Maybe he'll be sitting on my couch soon." He chuckled at his little joke.

Jenny said good-bye and hurried out to the waiting room. Miss Gurney was standing at a cabinet against the back wall, filing away tape cassettes. She turned quickly when Jenny entered the room and picked up an envelope from the desk. "Here's the doctor's bill to take to your mother," she said.

Jenny took the bill and tucked it into her canvas bag.

"I like your hair. Such a pretty color," the receptionist said in her hoarse, scratchy voice.

"Thanks," Jenny said, returning Miss Gurney's smile.

"Dr. Gurney is such a wonderful man," Miss Gurney said, returning to the tape cabinet. "I — I mean, Dr. Schindler," she corrected herself quickly. "I was a patient of his, too."

"That's nice," Jenny said awkwardly. She didn't know quite how to respond. "Uh . . . see you next time," she said, and quickly walked out of the office.

Her friends Claire and Rick were waiting for her at the mall, at the Pizza Oven. A large pepperoni pizza was on the table, several slices already devoured.

"Thanks for waiting, guys," Jenny said, rolling her eyes. She slid into the red vinyl booth beside Claire.

"Rick was starving," Claire explained, wiping tomato sauce off her chin with a paper napkin.

"Claire was starving," Rick explained, shoving the pizza tray toward Jenny. "It's still warm." He grinned at her, his wide grin.

Claire and Rick were Jenny's new friends, friends she had made after the horrifying events involving the Hagens. She had known Claire since elementary school, but they had never been close until now. Rick had been a longtime buddy of Claire's. Now they formed a very comfortable trio.

Rick was a big, good-looking jock with curly black hair and a goofy smile. Claire was as serious as Rick was unserious. She was very tall and thin, nearly a foot taller than Jenny, and had straight brown hair, which she usually wore behind her in a single braid, and serious brown eyes. She wasn't really pretty, but she would be one day. A lot of boys made fun of her because she was so tall.

Jenny liked Claire, she realized, because she was so serious.

Claire seldom made jokes. She almost never "got" jokes. She was serious and caring and sympathetic, which was more of what Jenny needed. These days, she often didn't feel like being teased or kidding around.

"Chuck was here," Claire said. "He said he was looking for you."

Jenny sighed. "He just doesn't give up."

"Chuck's a good guy," Rick said, just to annoy Jenny.

"Then *you* go out with him!" Jenny cracked.

"He's not my type," Rick said, reaching for another pizza slice.

"I'm glad you guys could meet me on your lunch break," Jenny said, changing the subject. Claire and Rick both had summer jobs at Rick's uncle's shoe store in the mall.

"It's nice to talk to someone who doesn't smell

like sneakers," Rick said and laughed at his own joke.

"How's it going?" Claire asked, sounding concerned.

"Oh, okay, I guess," Jenny said with a shrug. "I started that baby-sitting job Tuesday night."

"And?" Claire asked eagerly. She and Rick both knew how important the job was to Jenny.

"And the kid turns out to be this ten-year-old evil genius brat," Jenny said.

"Oh, wow," Claire said. "Is he really a terror?"

"Well, listen to this," Jenny said. "He raises tarantulas."

"Gross," Claire declared.

"You sure know how to pick 'em!" Rick said, and then looked very embarrassed, having realized what he said.

"Maybe you should quit this job and find another one," Claire suggested.

"Yeah. You could come help us lace sneakers all day," Rick said.

Jenny shook her head and swallowed a large chunk of cheese. "No. I'm going to try and stick it out. I think it would be good for me to try to stay with it. And the money's really good." She shrugged. "After all, what's a few tarantulas? Maybe they'll keep me on my toes."

Rick laughed and Claire forced a smile. They talked about the coming school year for a while, naming the teachers they hoped to get and the teachers they hoped to avoid. Then they talked about Rick's unsuccessful attempts to persuade his parents to buy him his own car.

"Uh-oh, we're going to be late," Claire said, staring at her watch as if it couldn't be telling the truth.

"Oh, no! If we're late, Uncle Bill will take away my shoehorn!" Rick declared with exaggerated horror. He slid out of the booth and jumped to his feet.

Jenny grabbed her bag and slid out so Claire could get out. "What are *you* going to do now?" Claire asked.

"Oh, I don't know. Wander around the mall, look at clothes, I guess," Jenny said, glancing toward the door. She half expected to see Chuck lurking there, waiting to spring on her, but he wasn't there. "If I stick with this job, I'll actually be able to afford some new clothes for school."

"Well, see you around," Rick said, giving her a little wave. He and Claire walked through the crowded restaurant and out the door, hurrying back to the shoe store, which was at the far end of the mall.

Jenny took a last slurp of her Coke, then wandered out into the brightly lit mall filled with midday shoppers, mostly housewives pushing strollers. Across from the restaurant, a new Buick revolved on a circular platform. BIG DRAWING ON SATURDAY, a Day-Glo-blue-and-orange sign proclaimed.

She looked through a couple of small clothing boutiques, then walked aimlessly through Sutton's, the large two-leveled department store in the center of the mall.

She pulled a few blouses off the rack and studied a very short, black suede skirt for a while. But her mind wasn't on shopping. She was thinking of her session with Dr. Schindler, of the things she had told him about her first encounter with Eli, of her feelings about how she had handled — or mishandled — the whole tarantula incident.

It was always hard to push the sessions with Dr. Schindler out of her mind. They seemed to follow her out of his office and stay with her, bits of conversation and thoughts swirling about, refusing to fade away, forcing her to sift through what she had said over and over again.

Whenever she saw the doctor, she felt unsettled for the rest of the day. It was as if their conversations stirred up all of her troubling thoughts, stirred up her imagination, which really didn't *need* stirring up, causing her to feel jumpy and out-of-sorts for many hours after the session ended.

Without realizing it, she had wandered into Blasters, the record store. It was a long, narrow store with hot red walls lined with big posters of music performers and a single aisle that led all the way to the back of the store, shelves of CDs on one side, cassettes on the other.

She bent down to look at some rap cassettes, then moved down the aisle to the pop-rock section. She was returning a cassette to its shelf when she noticed the boy watching her.

Glancing down the aisle at him, then quickly looking back at the cassettes, she saw that he was sort of tough-looking. He had short, spiky blond hair, so light it was almost platinum, and he was wearing black denim jeans and a red-and-black Aerosmith T-shirt.

He came closer, loping down the narrow aisle, taking big strides with his long legs.

Is he staring at me? Jenny wondered. She took a few steps toward the back of the store, then glanced back at him. He had a gold stud in one ear, she saw. And he had blue eyes.

Blue eyes that continued to look at her.

Yes, yes. He's staring at me. But why?

He continued to lope nearer, staring boldly.

Suddenly frightened, Jenny turned and began to walk quickly along the aisle toward the back.

What does he want? she wondered.

Why is he coming after me?

Is he coming after me? He looks so tough. Is he just trying to scare me?

There was no back exit to the store. Looking desperately around, Jenny realized that she was about to be trapped at the end of the aisle.

There was no one else around.

The lone sales clerk was at the register up near the front door, completely out of view.

The tough-looking blond boy came after her, his blue eyes now riveted to hers. Jenny saw that he had a scar along the bottom of his chin.

What does he want?

Why is he coming after me?

She was against the back wall now. Nowhere to run.

I'm trapped, she thought.

Completely trapped.

He wasn't stopping. He was coming for her.

Chapter 5

"You dropped this," he said.

Jenny's mouth fell open. "What?"

He handed her a small white envelope. It was the bill from Dr. Schindler's office. "It dropped out of your bag. When you bent down to look at cassettes."

Feeling like a complete fool, Jenny struggled to force her breathing back to normal and stop her pounding heartbeat, and reached out for the envelope. Once again, her wild imagination had led her down the wrong path.

"Thanks," she said. She knew her face was bright red. He must think I'm a real dweeb, she thought.

His sky-blue eyes did seem to be laughing at her. "I've never been in this store," he said.

"It's pretty good," Jenny said, still feeling embarrassed and uncomfortable. "But they have a bigger selection at Hit Power. It's across the street from the mall."

She wanted to get out of there, but he was blocking her way. He smelled of cinnamon for some reason. Jenny tried not to stare at the scar on his chin, but it was hard to avoid looking at it.

He's actually very good-looking, she thought. Although he does seem to be enjoying some private joke. His eyes seem to be laughing all the time.

"You live here?" he asked.

"You mean in the store?"

They both laughed. Nervous laughter. He looks like a little boy when he laughs, Jenny thought.

"I meant this town," he said, his blue eyes seeming to twinkle in the bright store light.

"Yeah," she said.

"I just moved here. A few weeks ago." He shifted his weight, then leaned against the display rack, still blocking the aisle. "Where do you go to school?"

"Harrison," Jenny told him.

"Hey, I'll be starting there in the fall."

I really like his smile, Jenny thought.

"It's not a bad school," she said, stuffing the envelope back into her canvas bag. "It's kinda big, though. I mean, if you're used to a smaller school."

"I'm used to a lot of schools," he said, growing serious, the laughter fading from his eyes. "My family travels around a lot. I'm sort of an army brat. Except my dad isn't in the army."

"That makes sense," Jenny cracked.

They both laughed again.

"Are you into Aerosmith?" she asked, making a face as she stared at his red-and-black T-shirt.

"No. I used to work in a T-shirt store," he said.

"This is one that nobody wanted, so I got it half-price."

Jenny laughed. "You're joking, right?"

He laughed, too. "No, I'm serious." He looked back down the long, narrow aisle, which was still empty except for the two of them, then turned back to her. "You hate heavy metal, huh?"

"Well . . . I used to like Def Leppard a little." Jenny took a step forward, trying to indicate to him that she wanted to leave. She realized she was feeling trapped.

"My name's Cal," he said.

"I'm Jenny. It was nice to meet you, Cal. I've got to get home now."

He stepped aside so that she could pass. Jenny started up the aisle, then realized he was following right behind.

"Hey, Jenny — "

She kept walking. She was nearly up to the front now. "I've really got to go," she called back to him.

He followed her out of the store. They stopped just outside the open doorway. A group of laughing teenagers hurried by, on their way to the movie sixplex just around the corner.

"Jenny — "

"Cal, really — "

"You wouldn't go out with me Friday night, would you?" he asked shyly, his hands jammed into his pockets. For once, he didn't look her in the eyes. Instead he stared past her at the kids heading to the movie theater.

"I don't know you. I — " Jenny stammered.

"This guy in my neighborhood, he goes to Harrison. Maybe you know him. Jim somebody."

"Jim Somebody?" Jenny joked. "Never heard of him."

"Jim . . . I don't remember," Cal said, scratching the back of his head. "Anyway, he invited me to a party Friday night. Maybe you could come with me, or something."

"I can't," Jenny said, shaking her head. "I have to baby-sit Friday night. I have this regular baby-sitting job, see."

"Hey, I meant *Saturday* night," Cal said, slapping his forehead. "Did I say Friday? No. I meant Saturday." He flashed her a warm smile. "You probably don't go out with guys you just meet at a mall, huh?"

"Well, I never have before," Jenny told him, shifting her bag to the other shoulder.

His grin grew wider. He still had his hands jammed into his pockets. "I'm not a bad guy. Really," he said. "Why not take a chance? Come to the party with me Saturday night. If you hate it after ten minutes, I'll take you right home. Promise."

Those eyes. Those incredible, pale blue eyes. Why did they always seem to be laughing at her?

Jenny stared into Cal's eyes, thinking hard, trying to decide.

Should she take a chance?

Should she go out with him?

"Got to run. We're a little late," Mr. Wexner said, picking up his sports jacket from the banister. Then he shouted up the stairs, " 'Bye, Eli. Have fun with Jenny!"

Mrs. Wexner came hurrying down the stairs, buttoning the sleeves of her blouse. "Hi, Jenny. How are you?" she asked, picking up her purse from the low table by the doorway. "Eli's watching TV upstairs," she said, before Jenny could answer. "He's been in a cranky mood all day. I'm sorry." She shook her head. "Just try to go along with him tonight. You know — go with the flow."

"I'm sure Jenny can handle Eli," her husband said. He chuckled, but his tone was tense and scolding. "Eli isn't really a monster, you know," he added, rolling his eyes. "You're going to frighten Jenny away."

"Oh, right," Mrs. Wexner snapped. "Like I frightened away all the other baby-sitters. I suppose it was my fault."

Mr. Wexner avoided Jenny's gaze. He looked very embarrassed.

"Why do you always have to defend Eli?" Mrs. Wexner continued angrily. "Why don't you defend *me* once in a while? That kid drove me crazy all day, and you want to ignore it and pretend he's a perfect angel!"

"Rena — *please*!" her husband pleaded. "Can we continue this discussion later? *Much* later?"

He gave Jenny a quick wave, his face filled with

embarrassment and annoyance. "See you later," he said wearily.

"Good luck," Mrs. Wexner added. And the two of them headed toward the back door.

Sounds like I'm in for a thrilling evening, Jenny thought. She dropped her bag by the living room couch and, taking a deep breath, headed up the stairs to Eli's room.

She found him sitting on his bed in the dark, watching some kind of horror film on a TV set a few inches away from the foot of his bed. "Hi, Eli. I'm back."

He didn't look up.

"What are you watching?"

"TV."

At least he answered me, she thought.

"Can I watch it with you?" she asked, moving toward the edge of his bed.

"If you want. Watch this." He pointed to the screen. "This guy's gonna get killed." He said it gleefully, an eager smile on his face.

Sure enough, the guy on the screen walked into a cabin and had his head cut off.

Yuck, Jenny thought, turning away to avoid seeing the blood splattering all over the cabin walls.

She watched Eli's reaction, his pale face reflecting the red from the TV screen. He started to giggle, then laugh out loud.

He thinks it's hilarious, Jenny realized with sudden revulsion.

"Eli — do you think you should be watching this

movie?" she asked. On the screen, a deranged-looking man was running through the woods carrying an ax.

"Who's gonna stop me?" Eli asked, challenge in his voice.

"I just mean — "

"I can watch whatever I want," he said angrily, his eyes not leaving the screen. "It's *my* room."

I don't want to turn this into a battle, Jenny thought, watching the man with the ax start chopping away at a teenage girl who looked a lot like Jenny.

Eli started laughing again, a high-pitched, gleeful laugh.

Is that what Eli would like to do to me? Jenny thought. Chop me to bits with an ax?

He's enjoying this awful flick way too much.

"I didn't have a good day," he said suddenly, turning away from the screen to look at her. The red and blue from the TV danced across his face, making him look like some kind of multicolored creature.

"I'm sorry," Jenny said sympathetically. "What was the problem?"

He thought about it for a moment. "My parents don't like my pets."

I can understand why! Jenny thought. But she didn't say it.

"I'm sorry," she said again. "Maybe you and I could have some fun tonight. Why don't you turn off the TV, and we'll — "

"No way." He turned his attention back to the screen.

"Come on, Eli. Let's play a game or something," she pleaded.

He ignored her, staring straight ahead at the screen.

"Eli — "

He continued to ignore her.

"Okay then. I'm going downstairs. I don't want to watch this horrible movie."

"It isn't horrible," he insisted. "It's good."

"See you later. I'm going downstairs."

He didn't reply.

She turned and walked out of the dark bedroom. As she reached the hallway, she heard him shrieking with laughter again, most likely at another hideous murder.

She went down to the living room, pulled the copy of *Sassy* she had brought out of her bag, and sat down in the big leather armchair to read.

As she flipped through the pages, she found herself thinking of Cal. Why on earth had she agreed to go to the party with him Saturday night?

I've never done that before, Jenny thought, feeling very uneasy. I don't know a thing about him. He seems sort of tough, not my type at all.

Why did I say yes?

Then she abruptly changed sides in the argument with herself. Why not take a chance? she asked herself. What have you got to lose?

She was still thinking about Cal when the phone

on the table beside her rang. Startled, it took her a few seconds to realize what the sound was.

Her heart was still pounding when she picked up the receiver. "Hello?"

The voice on the other end was just a whisper. *"Hi, Babes. I'm back."*

Chapter 6

There was a loud click, and the line went dead in her hand. Jenny clutched the receiver tightly, so tightly her hand hurt, hearing the whispered words again and again.

Hi, Babes. I'm back.

My nightmare is coming true.

That was her first thought.

The terrifying dream that she had had night after night. The dream in which Mr. Hagen came back for his revenge.

But it's impossible, she told herself, still clutching the phone receiver.

He's dead.

Mr. Hagen is dead.

I saw him fall over the quarry edge, down to the rocks below. I heard the *splat* his body made when it hit. I heard the *crack*.

I'll hear it as long as I live.

It *can't* be Mr. Hagen. People don't come back from the dead.

Do they?

The receiver started to buzz loudly in her hand. She returned it to the phone with a trembling hand.

"Hi, Babes. I'm back."

It wasn't a voice at all. It was just air, just wind.

Like a voice from beyond the grave. Like a voice a dead man would have, a dead man back from the grave.

It wasn't Mr. Hagen, Jenny told herself, gripping the arms of the chair. The magazine slid from her lap, but she didn't bother to pick it up.

But if it *wasn't* Mr. Hagen, how did he know the same words? The same exact words Mr. Hagen had used all those times he called to terrify Jenny?

"Hi, Babes." That's just what Mr. Hagen had said, whispered just the way he had whispered.

"This can't be happening to me again!" Jenny cried aloud.

Suddenly she was back in her dream, the dream that caused her to wake up screaming every morning.

There she was, back at the rock quarry, surrounded by blackness, blacker than the blackest night. There she was, staring at the gaping hole beyond the rock ledge, unable to move, unable to turn away, unable to leave.

Staring, staring at the black emptiness as the hand appeared on the quarry edge. First one hand, then the other. Mr. Hagen was pulling himself up.

His head appeared, the skin torn off one side of his face, pale skeleton showing through from underneath. One eye was missing, the gaping, empty socket bulging with pulsating veins.

Now Mr. Hagen pulled himself to his feet. One arm lay limp at his side. He shuffled toward her, pulling one leg stiffly as he moved, seeming to stare at her with the empty eye socket.

"Hi, Babes. I'm back."

"No! No!" Jenny jumped out of the chair, shaking her head hard, as if trying to shake away the dream.

It was *only* a dream after all. Only a nightmare.

And nightmares don't come true.

I'll go upstairs and see what Eli is doing, she decided.

She started walking toward the stairway, but stopped.

A sound.

It was coming from the kitchen.

She froze, listening hard.

It was the sound of the back door opening.

"Hi, Babes. I'm back." The whispered words repeated in her mind.

She forced them away, forced herself to listen to the sounds from the kitchen.

Yes. Yes. She hadn't imagined it.

She heard the kitchen door open.

And now, someone was walking through the kitchen.

Someone was about to find her, standing there, frozen in fear.

Chapter 7

"Mr. Wexner!" Jenny gasped.

"Sorry," he said, giving her an apologetic smile. "Hope I didn't startle you."

"No. I — I just didn't know who it was," Jenny said, wishing her heart would stop pounding so hard, wishing her voice didn't sound so high and frightened.

"Rena and I were so busy arguing when we left, I forgot the tickets," he said. He grabbed them up from the low table by the door. "What a night."

He started to leave, then poked his head back into the room from the doorway. "Everything okay here? Eli okay?"

"Yes. Fine," Jenny told him. "He's watching a horror movie. Do you usually let him watch really scary movies?"

Mr. Wexner sighed. "We really don't have much control over what he watches," he said.

"It's a pretty gory movie. I just wondered — " Jenny said.

"Well, maybe he'll get the blood and gore out of his system that way," Mr. Wexner said. "I've got to run." He disappeared to the kitchen. Jenny heard the back door slam behind him.

Get the blood and gore out of his system?

That's a strange thing to say, Jenny thought. She wondered if Mr. Wexner had any idea how much Eli enjoyed the blood-spattered murder scenes in the movie. How hard he laughed every time someone got killed.

Mr. Wexner's unexpected return had made Jenny forget about the frightening phone call for a minute.

It was obviously someone playing a very mean practical joke, Jenny decided. But who?

Puzzling about it, she climbed the stairs and peered into Eli's room. The TV had been turned off, to Jenny's surprise. The lights were on, and Eli was standing in the corner, staring into the glass cage that held his tarantulas.

"The movie over?" Jenny asked, walking up to him.

"No, but I didn't want to see the end," Eli said, his nose pressed against one side of the glass cage. Inside, three ugly, hairy tarantulas were scrambling over each other. "I don't like it when they kill the bad guy," Eli said, "so I turned it off."

He's definitely twisted, Jenny thought, her eyes on the scrabbling legs of the tarantulas.

"I've seen it four or five times already," Eli said. "I just fed my tarantulas. You missed it."

"What a shame," Jenny said sarcastically.

"They get all excited when I feed them. Just like real pets."

"Do they have names?" Jenny asked.

"That's babyish," he answered quickly, his eyes on the tarantulas.

Jenny glanced at the cat clock on the wall above the bed. Its tail was clicking back and forth, its eyes sliding right, then left in rhythm with the tail. "I like your clock," she said.

"It's babyish, too."

"Well, it may be babyish, but it's way past your bedtime," Jenny told him.

"Babyish," he said.

"Come on, Eli," she pleaded. "Don't give me a hard time — please."

"Babyish," he muttered, ignoring her plea. "I saw a movie on TV with a bunch of giant tarantulas. They were bigger than this house. They could eat you up in one bite."

"Yuck," she said, making a face.

It was the right reaction. He laughed.

"If I keep feeding mine, maybe they'll grow up to be giants, too."

What a sick mind, Jenny thought. "And who would you want your giant tarantulas to eat?" she asked.

"Everybody," he answered, without having to think about it.

Sweet, she thought. That's real sweet. "Come on, Eli. Bedtime. Go brush your teeth."

He yawned. "I'm not tired."

"Eli — no arguments," she said sternly, beginning to lose her patience.

"I'm not tired. Really," he whined, sounding like a little boy suddenly. "If I get into bed, can I read for a while?"

"Well . . ."

"Please please please please?"

Jenny laughed. "Okay. I guess. For a little while. What are you reading?"

He walked over to his counter, picked up a book, and returned with it. "This. It's really neat."

Jenny took it from him and stared at the title. "A Stephen King book? You're reading a Stephen King book?"

He shrugged. "So?"

"This one is supposed to be really gruesome," Jenny said. "Why don't you read something for kids your age?"

"Bor-ing," he said in a singsong voice, taking the Stephen King novel back from her.

It must be hard being ten and being so smart, Jenny realized. He can't really be a kid and read children's books and do other things normal ten-year-olds enjoy. But he can't really act like a grown-up, either.

"Will you tuck me in?" he asked sweetly.

Jenny quickly agreed, unable to stifle a laugh. Here he was, reading this gruesome horror novel, asking to be tucked into bed in a tiny voice.

Of course it took another half hour to actually

get him into bed. First he needed a drink of apple juice. Then he decided he was hungry and needed a bowl of cereal. Then he suddenly wanted to chat.

By the time Jenny got him tucked in, it was nearly eleven o'clock. The Wexners returned home a little before twelve, surprised to find Jenny sitting in the living room staring out the window into the darkness.

"Jenny, are you okay?" Mrs. Wexner asked.

"Yes. Fine," Jenny replied, jumping up from the chair. No point in telling them about the phone call, she decided.

"You look very tired," Mrs. Wexner said, her eyes studying Jenny's face. "I hope Eli didn't give you a hard time tonight."

"No. He was fine," Jenny told her, gathering up her backpack. "He watched a movie. Then he played with his spiders."

Mrs. Wexner made a face. "Those disgusting tarantulas. I'm so sorry I let him talk us into getting them for him. He said it was for a science fair at school. But then he got so attached to them, he wouldn't let us get rid of them."

"They're not the *cutest* pets in the world," Jenny said, laughing.

"I'm glad he wasn't . . . difficult," Mrs. Wexner said.

Wow, Jenny thought. Eli must be a real terror sometimes. His mother seems totally amazed that I'm not ready to quit already.

Just how bad *is* the kid?

"Want me to drive you home?" Mr. Wexner asked, appearing in the doorway.

"No. No, thanks," Jenny replied. "It's such a short walk. There's no need."

"Are you sure?" Mrs. Wexner asked, her face filled with concern. "It's so late."

"I'll be home in less than five minutes," Jenny assured her. "Really. I'll be fine."

A few minutes later, adjusting her backpack on her shoulders, she stepped out into the night. It was surprisingly warm and still. A half moon hovered above the trees in a smooth cloudless sky.

Her sneakers crunched loudly down the gravel drive. There were no other sounds. The other houses on the block were all dark.

People go to bed early around here, she thought, turning at the foot of the driveway, following the street toward her house. She had a sudden chill. For no reason at all.

Or *was* there a reason?

What was that sound?

Footsteps on the grass?

The sound was so close. Right behind her.

Someone was there.

She spun around and saw him.

He grabbed her before she had a chance to scream.

"Jenny — I've been waiting for you."

Chapter 8

Jenny's mouth dropped open in a silent gasp of surprise. She struggled to find her voice.

"Jenny—I've been waiting for you."

He gripped her shoulders tightly.

"Chuck—what are you *doing* here? Let *go* of me!" she cried.

She tried to pull away from him, but he refused to let go.

His eyes were wild. His blond hair was in disarray. The front of his sleeveless T-shirt was stained with sweat.

He's so big and strong, she thought. He could crush me if he wanted to. "Let go!" she insisted.

"Not until you agree to talk to me," he said, holding on tightly to her shoulders.

"You're *hurting* me!" she cried.

He let go, but didn't step back. His chest heaved. His breath felt hot on her face.

"Chuck — what are you doing? What do you want?"

63

"I just want to talk, that's all," he said, breathlessly, staring into her eyes as if searching for something inside them, something that was no longer there.

"You — you really frightened me," Jenny said, taking a step back along the low curb.

It suddenly grew darker. She turned and saw that the Wexners had just turned off their porch light.

"Why won't you talk to me?" Chuck insisted, his voice a loud whisper.

"There isn't anything to talk about," Jenny said, calming a little, still watching his face warily.

"Don't say that!" he shouted angrily. "Stop saying that!"

"But, Chuck — "

"Why won't you give me a chance?"

"I've explained to you."

"You haven't explained anything." He took a step toward her. Was he trying to frighten her?

"You're supposed to be Mr. Jokes," she said. "Always cracking everyone up. What's happened to your sense of humor, Chuck? Why are you acting like this is such a tragedy?"

"Do *you* think it's funny?" he asked accusingly, his eyes growing wild again. "It's just a joke to you?" His face filled with anger.

"No — that's not what I said," Jenny cried.

"You were the best thing that ever happened to me," he said, his eyes burning into hers. "And then, you dumped me. No explanation."

"No explanation?" she cried. "Chuck, I went through a nightmare. I was being stalked by a crazy man. I was responsible for that man being killed. My life was like a horror movie. Afterward, I needed a change. A complete change. I'm still haunted by . . . by everything that happened. I still can't get rid of that nightmare. What *more* of an explanation do I have to give you?"

He didn't reply. Just stared at her, his features tight with anger.

"I'm sorry," she said, her voice cracking. "Sorry if I hurt you. But . . . but I can't stand to be reminded of what happened. And you — you — "

"I remind you of what happened? Jenny, I was there for you. I was there for you when you needed me. And now — you repay me by — by — " He was so angry, he couldn't speak.

Taking another step back, Jenny had a sudden, frightening thought. "Chuck — did you call me tonight?" she asked.

Was he the one?

Was he the one who called and said, "Hi, Babes. I'm back"?

It *could* have been Chuck, she realized. It *could* have been him. Who else knew Mr. Hagen's exact words?

"Did you call me?"

"Yes," he admitted, his anger not cooling.

"You *did*?!" she cried. "You called me at the Wexners'?"

"Huh?"

"You were the one?"

"Whoa," he said, raising a hand as if to hold her back. "I called you at your house. Your mother told me where you were."

"And you didn't call me at the Wexners'?"

"Don't change the subject!" he screamed.

She tried to read his expression, tried to read his eyes, to determine if he was the one who had tried to terrify her. But she could see only anger there.

"Chuck — I want to go home now." Her words, spoken so softly, seemed to hover in the still night air.

"No! You can't! You've got to stay. We've got to talk."

She couldn't fight the tears back any longer. They ran down her cheeks, hot and sticky. "Chuck — please. What more can I say? It's over. Just face it. I'm so sorry. But it's over."

"No!" he screamed, in a rage.

He grabbed her shoulders hard.

"Chuck — let go — "

She jerked away, tried to free herself. But he was so strong, and his rage seemed to make him even stronger.

"No!"

"Chuck — what are you going to do?" Her voice revealed her fear.

He was out of control, she realized. Completely out of control.

"No! No! Let *go*!!"

With a loud groan, he heaved her down onto the pavement.

"Ow!" she cried out as the back of her head hit the curb. "What are you doing? What are you going to do to me?"

He stood above her, breathing noisily.

Is he going to kill me? Jenny wondered.

This isn't happening, she thought, the back of her head throbbing with pain, her thoughts swirling in her mind. This isn't Chuck. Chuck was always so lovable, so . . . funny.

What have I done to him?

What is he going to do to me?

"Chuck — "

He was standing above her, gulping air.

She tried to sit up. She felt dizzy at first, but it passed quickly.

"Chuck, I have to know — was it you who called me tonight?"

He didn't reply.

She climbed unsteadily to her feet. "Chuck — "

"You'll be sorry," he whispered, still breathing hard. He was looking past her now, off into the dark trees across the street.

"Chuck, I've got to know — "

"You'll be sorry, Jenny."

Then, without looking at her, he turned and ran.

Tears drying on her face, her head throbbing, she stood and watched him run. He turned the corner, running at full speed. His car was parked under the trees. She saw the light go on as he opened the car door, saw him climb into the car, shielded her eyes as the headlights flashed on, and the car squealed away, following its own white rectangle of light.

She waited until his car was out of sight, until she could no longer hear the roar of its engine, and then she began walking toward her home, taking long but unsteady strides.

He hates me so much, she realized.

I hurt him so much.

I hurt him. He hates me.

The words repeated and repeated, followed her home, followed her up the stairs to her room, followed her into the shower.

I hurt him. He hates me.

The words followed her into her bed, wouldn't let her get to sleep. Wouldn't let her think about anything else.

I hurt him. He hates me.

She had almost drifted off when the phone beside her bed rang.

She reached out her hand and grabbed the receiver.

Should she pick it up?

Despite the heat of the night, she suddenly felt cold all over.

Cold dread.

It rang a second time.

If I don't pick it up, it'll wake Mom, she thought.

But I don't want to pick it up.

I don't want to hear that whispered voice again, that whispered voice from the grave. . . .

She picked up the receiver and raised it to her ear. "Hello?"

There it was. The whispered voice on the other end.

"Jenny? It's me."

Chapter 9

"What — what do you want?" Jenny cried, sitting up in her bed, the covers slipping to the floor.

"*Jenny — it's me.*" The whispered voice, followed by a high-pitched giggle.

Her room seemed to tilt, first to one side, then the other. "Chuck — why are you doing this?" She was so frightened, she didn't recognize her own voice, so hoarse, so tight.

Another whispered giggle. Followed by crackling static on the line. Then: "*Jenny — it's me. Eli.*"

"What?"

She hadn't heard correctly — had she?

Was her mind playing tricks on her? Had she scrambled her brains when she bumped her head against the pavement?

"It's Eli," came the little boy's whispered voice. "I'm calling on the phone I made." Another hushed giggle.

"Eli — it's you?"

She could hear him breathing on the other end.

"Eli?"

"Isn't this *neat*?" he asked in his normal voice, forgetting to whisper.

"Eli — why are you calling me?"

"Mom and Dad don't know," he said. "It's so awesome! My phone really works!"

"Awesome," Jenny repeated, her heartbeat starting to return to normal. She reached down and pulled the covers up off the floor. "Listen, Eli — it's very late."

"I know."

"And I'm coming to baby-sit for you all day tomorrow. So how about hanging up, and we'll both get some sleep?" Jenny didn't mean to sound as annoyed as she did, but he really had frightened her. And after her run-in with Chuck, she didn't need another scare that night.

"I can call you whenever I want," Eli said, ignoring her request. "Isn't that awesome?"

If he says "awesome" one more time, I'll be forced to murder him, Jenny thought.

"I'm going to hang up now, Eli," she said, yawning. "Good night." She replaced the receiver and glanced at the clock on her bed table. Nearly two-thirty. What on earth was Eli doing up at two-thirty?

Phoning her, of course!

She was still trying to rearrange the covers when the phone rang again.

Another stab of terror.

This time . . . this time . . . who would it be?

She picked up the receiver before the second ring. "Hello?"

"Hi. You didn't let me say good night."

"Eli — get off the phone! Go to sleep!"

He sounded very hurt. "I just wanted to say good night."

"Well, good night."

"Good night, Jenny." He giggled and hung up.

What an evil giggle, she thought.

It took her nearly half an hour to finally fall into a light, dreamless sleep.

"Great party," Jenny said, rolling her eyes sarcastically.

"Glad you're into it," Cal said, grinning.

Someone had turned off the lights in the living room, and couples were sprawled all over the floor. There were couples making out in the den, too. And in the dining room, some guys who had somehow gotten hold of a keg of beer were puzzling over it, trying to figure out how to get the tap to work. Rap music boomed from speakers set up all over the house.

Cal was wearing black, straight-legged jeans and an oversized, short-sleeved Hawaiian shirt. Jenny wore a green T-shirt over an orange sleeveless T-shirt over white tennis shorts. It was hard to tell what anyone else at the party was wearing. It was too dark!

Cal clasped Jenny's hand as they looked in vain for a quiet place to sit down. "How about the front

yard?" Jenny said, leaning against Cal and screaming over the music.

Cal tripped over a couple entangled on the living
room carpet and would have fallen if Jenny hadn't
held onto him. They both laughed.

"Where's the guy you said invited you to this?"
Jenny asked.

"What? I can't hear you."

"Where's our host?"

"I don't know." Cal shrugged. "Maybe he's here.
I don't really remember what he looks like."

"Come on," Jenny said, tugging his arm. "This
isn't exactly my kind of party." She pulled him toward the front hallway.

"But it's just getting started," he protested.

She dropped his arm. "You're not serious. You
really want to stay?"

He shook his head. "No. Let's go."

They stumbled out the front door and hurried
out of the house. Two guys with long, greased-down
hair, both wearing denim jackets over plain white
T-shirts, came swaggering up the walk. "This where
the party is?" one of them asked Cal while the other
looked Jenny up and down.

"No. It's next door," Cal said with a straight face,
pointing.

"Thanks, man." The two of them turned and
headed across the lawn to the house Cal had pointed
to.

"Poor neighbors," Jenny whispered. "What a
mean joke."

"Let's get out of here," Cal said, grinning as he pulled Jenny to his car, a scratched-up Dodge Dart that had seen better days.

He was still smiling as he started up the car, hurriedly backed down the drive, and then squealed away. But as soon as they were a few blocks from the party, Jenny noticed that his mood had changed.

His smile had faded, replaced by a grim thoughtfulness. He drove in silence, his eyes straight ahead on the road.

"Hey," Jenny called, sliding a bit closer to him. "Where are we going?"

He didn't answer, didn't seem to hear her.

"Hey, Cal — yoo-hoo!" she called, confused. "What's wrong?"

He shrugged, his expression unchanging. He ran his finger slowly along the scar on his chin.

What's going on here? Jenny wondered. One minute he's laughing and playing practical jokes. The next minute he's as quiet and somber as a tomb!

"Cal?"

"Sorry," he said, his spiked hair shining, his eyes suddenly flashing bright blue as they drove under a streetlight. "It's just that I — I'm so . . . embarrassed."

Jenny wasn't sure she heard him correctly.

"What did you say?"

"I'm embarrassed, that's all." He said it with a flash of anger.

"I don't get it."

"I wanted to show you a good time," he said,

staring straight ahead, avoiding her glance. "You know, impress you. But instead I took you to that stupid party with a bunch of creeps acting like animals."

Jenny couldn't help but laugh. "I've been to wild parties before, you know."

Her laughter seemed to make him more upset.

"I just wanted to make a good impression, that's all," he said. "Instead, there we were, stumbling around in the dark with a bunch of dorks who couldn't figure out how to work a beer keg."

Jenny started to make a joke, but stopped when she saw how upset Cal was. "Just forget about it," she said, touching his hand.

"I can't," he insisted, frowning and looking away.

"It's no big deal," she said. "Come on, Cal. I spent the entire day with a ten-year-old who thought everything I suggested we do was too boring and too babyish. No matter *what* we do tonight, it's got to be an improvement on that!"

"Oh, that makes me feel a *lot* better," he said, sounding like a child himself.

"Pull over," Jenny said suddenly.

His expression changed to one of surprise. "What?"

"Pull over," Jenny urged. "Right now."

"You're getting out?" he asked. "We're in the middle of nowhere. At least let me drive you home — "

"Will you just pull over?!" Jenny insisted.

He obediently swung the car to the curb,

stopped, and pushed the gearshift to park. Then he turned to her. "Listen, I'm real sorry — "

Before he could finish his sentence, she flung herself across the seat onto him, threw her arms around his shoulders, and pressed her lips against his in a long, hard kiss.

"Okay," she said when the kiss had come to an end, "you can go on driving now."

"Jenny — "

"I've been wanting to do that all night," Jenny said, feeling really happy for the first time in many months. "I guess you made a good impression on me after all, Cal."

She started to settle back into her seat, but he grabbed her, pulled her back to him, and kissed her again. This time, he wouldn't let the kiss end.

He's so . . . needy, Jenny thought, kissing him back, her eyes shut tight. Maybe that's what we have in common. Maybe that's why I feel so attracted to him, even though I hardly know a thing about him.

We're *both* so needy.

She pulled away from him. "Cal — we'd better stop."

He looked disappointed. She settled back in her seat, straightening her T-shirt. Her heart was pounding. She wanted to kiss him again. And again. And again.

So needy. . . .

"It's still early," she said. "Why don't we do something?"

He smiled at her, his blue eyes sparkling from the light of a streetlight above them. He reached for the gearshift on the steering column and slid it back into drive.

"I know! Let's go skating!" Jenny said.

"Roller skating?"

"Yeah. There's a rink just past Halsey Manor — you know, on the North Road."

"But we don't have skates," he protested.

"They rent them, silly," she said.

For a brief second, his eyes went cold, his expression hardened.

Jenny caught the change of expression and immediately understood. He doesn't like to be called "silly," she realized.

He certainly is sensitive, she thought.

She started to apologize, but his expression had softened, his smile returned. "Do you skate?" she asked, staring at him as he drove, dark trees and hedges rolling past the car windows in a shadowy blur.

"I'm willing to give it a try," he said.

"You mean you've never skated in your life?" she exclaimed.

He shrugged. "I've had a tough life."

She stared into his eyes, trying to determine how seriously he meant that. But she couldn't tell.

Headlights from an oncoming car suddenly illuminated them both, as if a spotlight had been turned on them. In the sudden brightness, Jenny was struck by how tough Cal looked, how hard. The silver stud in his ear glistened, and his short, spiked hair glowed white and then faded back into shadows as the oncoming car passed by.

What am I *doing* here with this boy, this tough-looking stranger? Jenny asked herself.

Enjoying yourself. Having a good time. For once.

She answered her own question.

"Come on, Cal — turn here. The skating rink is right over this hill. It'll be fun."

"Fun," he repeated uncertainly, but he obediently turned and headed toward the rink.

The rink was crowded, and noisy, and . . . fun. An endless stream of rock and dance music flowed from the enormous speakers on the rafters. Jenny had trouble at first. She hadn't skated in quite a while, and one of her rented skates had a wheel that kept sticking.

To his own surprise, Cal turned out to be a natural skater. He whirled around the rink with ease. He was so good, Jenny accused him of having skated before. He laughed in reply, and explained that he was just a natural athlete.

Again, she couldn't tell if he was serious or not. It was so hard to tell when he was putting her on. But she didn't care. She really liked him.

She didn't want the evening to end. But at a little past midnight, he pulled up her driveway, and then walked her up to the front porch.

They kissed under the porchlight, shyly this time. Too briefly, Jenny thought.

"See you soon," Cal said casually.

Then Jenny saw a hedge rustle at the side of the house.

Too fast, too hard to be the wind.

Someone's hiding there, she realized.

She grabbed Cal's arm. "Cal — look," she whispered, pointing.

The hedge moved again. She heard the crackle of dry leaves.

"Hey — who's there?" Cal shouted angrily.

The hedge shook in response, and they both heard shoes sliding over the dry, crackling leaves on the ground.

Then someone running hard.

"Hey — " Cal shouted. He took off in the direction of the footsteps, running at full speed.

"Stop!" Jenny cried. "Cal — come back!"

It could be . . . it could be . . . Mr. Hagen.

The thought flashed into her mind.

It could be Mr. Hagen, back from the dead, waiting for her in the darkness.

Stupid thought. But she couldn't help but think it.

"Cal — come back!"

He stopped. He turned and came jogging back to her.

Was it Chuck? she wondered.

"Someone was definitely hiding over there," he said, breathing hard. "Probably a burglar."

"Probably," she said.

A burglar. Of course. That was the normal thing to suspect.

But it hadn't even occurred to Jenny that it might be a burglar.

"You were very brave," she said.

"I was very stupid," he said, shaking his head.

"You're not stupid. Don't say that." She kissed him quickly on the cheek, surprising him, turned, and hurried into the house.

She made sure all the doors were locked, then ran up the stairs, turned off the hall light, and stood on the second-floor landing, listening to Cal's car roar off. She undressed quickly, forcing herself not to think about the person lurking behind the hedge. Instead, she thought about Cal, about what a good skater he was, about how sensitive he seemed, remembering how sullen and embarrassed he had become because of the party.

After changing into her oversized, black-and-white-striped nightshirt, she didn't feel at all tired. She pulled an old copy of *Seventeen* off her shelf, turned on the light over her headboard, and settled into bed to read for a while.

She was just beginning to feel drowsy when the phone rang.

She glanced at the clock on her night table — 1:17.

She grabbed up the receiver before it could ring a second time. "Listen, Eli — I told you not to call this late!"

"*It isn't Eli,*" said a hoarse, whispered voice.

Jenny's breath caught in her throat.

"*Jenny, I'm back.*"

"No! Stop it!" she managed to yell.

"Are you all alone, Babes?"

The same words Mr. Hagen had used.

"Leave me alone! This isn't funny!" Jenny cried. She was gripping the phone so tightly, her hand ached.

"Company's coming," whispered the voice.

Again, the words of Mr. Hagen's that had terrified her months before.

Why did the whispered voice sound so far away?

"Who *is* this? What do you *want*?"

Her questions were greeted by a crackle of static on the line. And then silence.

Chapter 10

Small puddles of water glistened across the pavement like hundreds of glowing eyes. The endless stretch of asphalt seemed to shimmer and gleam.

To Jenny's eyes, the rain had transformed the parking lot, washed away its solid reality, turned it into a dark, sparkling jewel spread out around her feet.

Nothing is real, she thought.

Not the darkened stores of the mall, not my car in this vast, empty parking lot, not this old-fashioned-style street lamp I'm standing under.

The rain has enchanted everything, like fairy dust. She let her eyes blur until everything seemed to come together as one glistening, dark light. Then she brought it all back into focus, scraped her wet sneakers against the pavement, and looked for Cal.

Where was he? He was supposed to meet her here at the far end of the Walker Mall parking lot. Behind the Doughnut Hole, he had said. Off in the back corner of the endless lot, back where they kept the large green bins for people to drop in old used clothing for some church charity.

The rain had stopped nearly fifteen minutes ago. Jenny had arrived early, had parked and watched the stores go dark, one by one, as if in a chain reaction. Then she had watched the last of the cars drive off into the glowing, wet darkness.

All alone on this unending parking lot. She had climbed out of the car, grateful for the fresh smell of the air, the cool dampness of it. It felt so good on her skin. The air was so wet that droplets formed in her hair.

Where's Cal?

She began to pace from her car to the clothing bins, under the yellow cone of light from the tall, curved street lamp.

It was late. Very late.

Why had she agreed to meet him so late at night? Why had she agreed on this strange, unearthly meeting place, this empty, cratered planet of a parking lot?

Because she wanted to see him.

Because he had asked her to meet him here.

I'm all alone, Jenny thought. I can do anything. I can dance. I can sing.

This whole, glowing, fresh world is mine!

She began to hum to herself as she paced from the car to the big green bins, then back again. It grew darker suddenly. The pavement lost its sparkle. Jenny looked up to see that a thick curtain of clouds had covered the moon.

There were no stars.

The sky was black and solid, tar-black.

She began to feel impatient.

It wasn't right of Cal to keep her waiting in this corner of the dark, empty lot.

It wasn't right.

She felt a drop of water on her forehead, cold and startling. Then a drop on her shoulder. It was beginning to rain again, a cold sprinkle.

Cal, where are you? Hurry, please.

You know I'm waiting out here for you.

She stopped when she heard the scraping sound. Where was it coming from?

Just the wind?

The wind didn't *scrape*, did it?

"Cal — is that you? Cal? Are you here?"

The parking lot was so dark. Most of the other street lamps were out for some reason. Knocked out by the rain, maybe.

Someone groaned. Very nearby.

"Cal?"

She felt a sudden, cold tremor of fear avalanche down her spine.

Something moved. Something scraped. Someone groaned. Again.

"Cal? Please!"

Her heart seemed to stop. She had to force herself to breathe.

Then, standing under the yellow light, the cold rain beginning to fall, standing halfway between the car and the clothing bins, she saw the hand, and then the arm.

"Ohh."

There was a hand sticking out of the clothing bin.

"No!"

Is it . . . Cal?

Has something horrible happened to Cal? Is that his hand, his arm?

Without thinking, without hesitating, she ran to the bin, pushed on the lid, grabbed the hand — so cold, such a cold hand — and pulled.

As she tugged, the cold hand came to life. It gripped her hand in an icy hold.

"Hey!" she cried.

She pulled, and the figure climbed out of the bin, emerged as if floating out. Still gripping her hand, he stepped under the light.

"No!" she screamed, struggling to free herself from his grasp.

"Please — *no!*"

He grinned at her, his face olive-green under the street lamp.

Mr. Hagen grinned at her. One eye was missing, revealing a dry, empty socket. His skull showed through where pieces of his cheek and forehead flesh had decayed and fallen off.

The stench. The stench was so strong. The stench swirled around him, swirled around both of them, holding her, drawing her toward him, not letting her run.

"Jenny — " he whispered, holding her so tightly in his icy grip.

When he opened his mouth to utter her name, she could see the gaps in his mouth, the rotting, black teeth.

"Jenny — " he repeated, his voice nothing but dry, rancid air.

A black bug crawled over his swollen tongue. He repeatedly licked his dry lips, but his tongue was dry and caked with dirt.

"No!" Jenny screamed. "Let me go! I'm *begging* you! You're dead! You're dead! Let me go!"

"Jenny — I'm back!"

Chapter 11

"Then I woke up, screaming my head off," Jenny said, twisting and untwisting a dark strand of hair. "Mom was already in my room, sitting on the edge of the bed, trying to wake me up, trying to get me out of that horrible dream."

Dr. Schindler cleared his throat, but didn't say anything. He fiddled with his desk clock, waiting for Jenny to continue.

"It was kind of the same dream I've had before," she said, "except it was in a different place. And it seemed more real somehow."

"More real?" the psychiatrist asked, his green eyes suddenly coming to life.

"Yes. All the rain. I could feel the rain, feel the dampness of the air. And the colors. And the smell." Jenny made a disgusted face, remembering. "I swear, Dr. Schindler, I could still smell the stench of Mr. Hagen, that smell of decay, of rotting meat, even after I woke up."

"A very vivid dream," Dr. Schindler muttered,

checking his tape player, then returning his glance to her. "You say it took place in a different location this time?"

"Yes. All the other times I dreamed it, I was at the rock quarry," Jenny said, nervously twisting the strand of hair. "Not at a mall parking lot. I don't know *why* I was at that parking lot."

The room was silent for a while. Jenny could hear the soft hum of the tape recorder and the bubble of water in the coffee maker across the room from her. She stared at Dr. Schindler's carefully lined-up diplomas on the wall, waiting for him to say something, wondering if he was waiting for her.

"Can you think of something *else* that's different about this dream?" he asked finally. It was obvious to her that he had something in mind. Why didn't he just *say* it? Why did he only ask questions and force *her* to do all the work?

"Something else different?" Jenny thought hard, staring at the diplomas until they blurred into one big diploma. "Well . . . I guess it's the first time Cal was in the dream."

"He wasn't really *in* the dream, was he?" the doctor asked quietly, leaning forward on the mahogany desk.

"Well, no. But he was the reason I was in the parking lot."

"He was the reason?"

"Yes," Jenny answered sharply. What was Dr. Schindler leading her to?

"Why do you think he was in your dream in this manner?" he asked her.

Jenny thought about it. "I don't know."

"Do you think maybe you're unsure about Cal?" Dr. Schindler asked. "Are you maybe unsure of his motives? Are you possibly a little suspicious of Cal?"

"I don't know. I don't *think* so," Jenny answered quickly, feeling confused.

"These frightening phone calls you were telling me about," the doctor continued. "Do you think that somewhere in your mind you might suspect Cal of making them?"

"Cal? No!" Jenny exclaimed. "How could I? I mean, how could *he*? How could Cal know what Mr. Hagen whispered to me when he made those frightening calls?"

"I'm just trying to get you to think about the dream," Dr. Schindler said, settling back in his big leather desk chair. "Tell me more about the phone calls."

"There isn't much more to tell," Jenny said, her mind whirling with too many thoughts at once. "I get them late at night. The same hoarse whisper. The same words. It — it's just so scary!"

Jenny sat up, hoping to clear her head. "Dr. Schindler — am I going crazy? These calls — "

"Sometimes after such a violent trauma," said the doctor, "our imagination doesn't settle down for a while."

"What?" Jenny jumped angrily to her feet.

"You — you think I *imagined* those phone calls?"

"Please let me finish," Dr. Schindler said calmly, motioning for her to resume her place on the couch. "I'm not trying to upset you, Jenny. But we have to think about these things very carefully and consider all kinds of possibilities."

Jenny was too angry and upset to sit down. She stood in front of the couch with her arms crossed tightly in front of her. "And you think the phone call I got the other night was all in my imagination?"

"I think the phone calls might be like your dreams," the doctor said, clasping the edge of his desk with both hands. "Your dreams are so vivid, so lifelike, you can even smell them. Who's to say that the same impulses that drive these dreams aren't also driving you to — ?"

"I don't understand what you're saying!" Jenny screamed.

He looked at his desk clock, raking his hand quickly through his coppery hair. "Our time is up for today. It's just as well, I believe. We need to be calm if we are to discuss this properly."

"How can I be calm?" Jenny cried.

She felt hurt. Betrayed, even.

Dr. Schindler obviously thought she was crazy!

How *could* she be imagining those terrifying phone calls?

They were real. They *had* to be real.

Or was she really cracking up?

"Would you like to schedule an extra session for

tomorrow?" Dr. Schindler asked, standing up, staring at her intently.

"An extra session?"

"If it would help make you feel better," he said, stretching.

"No. I can't," she said, her head spinning. "I have to baby-sit for Eli all day. I was there all morning, and I have to work tomorrow, too. The Wexners need me more often than they thought they would."

"How did it go with Eli this morning?" the doctor asked, walking her to the door.

"Not well. Eli was mad at me for some reason. I couldn't get him to tell me why. He said he hated me, then wouldn't say another word."

"You've had an upsetting day," Dr. Schindler said sympathetically. "Can I prescribe something to calm you? Some sleeping pills?" He opened the door to the waiting room with one hand and put his other hand on Jenny's shoulder. Miss Gurney looked up from her desk outside the door. "It really wouldn't hurt to take a sleeping pill tonight," he told Jenny softly.

"Okay," Jenny relented. "Maybe it's a good idea."

He walked her over to Miss Gurney's desk, his hand on her shoulder, and quickly scribbled a prescription in the illegible handwriting that all doctors share. He tore it off the pad and handed it to her with a warm smile, the first time Jenny had seen him smile all afternoon.

"A little sleep should help," he said, turning back

toward his office. "Please call me any time if you need to." He closed the door behind him.

Jenny collected her bag from the coat closet.

"You look tired today," Miss Gurney said, studying Jenny's face.

"I didn't sleep too well last night," Jenny replied. She said good-bye to the receptionist and headed out to the street.

It was a hot, humid afternoon, the sun still high in the sky. A wall of dark gray clouds appeared to be moving closer from the south. It was probably going to rain again.

Walking quickly down the hill to the bus stop, Jenny reached into her bag to see if she had remembered to bring bus fare.

To her surprise, she felt something prickly in her bag. Prickly and squishy.

Had something spilled?

What could it be?

She wrapped her hand around it and pulled it out of her bag.

Several people nearby on the sidewalk turned, startled, as Jenny screamed and dropped her bag.

She screamed again, staring at the dead tarantula in her hand.

Chapter 12

Jenny ran into the house, slamming the door behind her, tossed down her bag, and headed for the phone. She punched in the Wexners' number, her heart still pounding.

She couldn't overlook this horrid joke of Eli's. She had to tell Mrs. Wexner about it. For one thing, it was a really cruel joke for Eli to play on her, knowing that she was afraid of spiders. But more importantly, had he actually *killed* one of his pets just to play a joke?

His parents had to know about this, Jenny decided.

The phone rang once, twice. After the eighth ring, she slammed the receiver down in frustration. "YAAAAAAAII!" she screamed at the top of her lungs, knowing she was the only one home.

It didn't make her feel any better.

What a spectacle she had made of herself on the sidewalk near Dr. Schindler's office. There she was, shrieking like a crazy person, all of her belongings strewn about her feet, a dead tarantula in her hand.

Everyone on the sidewalk thought I was totally nuts, Jenny thought, shaking her head.

Maybe I *am* totally nuts.

Dr. Schindler thinks so, too. She thought of how he suggested that she might be imagining the whispered phone calls from Mr. Hagen and felt the anger well up inside her all over again.

Could he be right?

She had always had a wild imagination. Her fantasies and daydreams had often seemed as real to her as things that actually happened. And her dreams had always been vivid and lifelike.

But could she be so confused about what is real and what isn't that she fantasized those frightening phone calls and then believed them to be real?

Thinking about this was giving her a headache. She walked into the kitchen and took a Coke from the refrigerator. After several long gulps from the can, she glanced up at the clock over the stove. Four-thirty.

"Oh, no!" she cried aloud.

She was supposed to meet Claire and Rick at four-thirty at the tennis courts behind the high school. They were getting off work early so they could play a few games of tennis with her.

Jenny ran upstairs, grabbed her tennis racquet, looked at herself in the mirror, gave her tousled hair a quick brush, then hurried out of the house, planning to jog the three blocks to the school.

"Hey — Jenny!" a voice called at the foot of the drive.

She cried out, startled. "Cal — what are you doing here?"

"Just wanted to say hi," he said, running up to her and giving her a shy smile, his blue eyes burning into hers.

"I'm late," she said awkwardly. "I'm supposed to be playing tennis with my friends."

"Oh, I see." His face filled with disappointment.

"Hey — do you play?" she asked. "We could use a fourth, actually. Then we could play real doubles."

"I could give it a try," he said, smiling.

"That's what you said when I asked if you'd ever skated before," Jenny said, laughing. "And you turned out to be great at it."

"Beginner's luck," he said with a shrug. He was wearing a denim workshirt and faded jean cutoffs. Jenny thought he looked really great.

She ran back into the house and got a tennis racquet for him. They started together toward the school.

"Which end do you hold? This skinny part here?" Cal asked, flipping the racquet in his hands.

"Very funny," Jenny said, making a face.

"You're in a swell mood today," he said as they jogged across Henry Street. Jenny waved to Mrs. Russell, out pulling up weeds as usual.

"Oh, you noticed," Jenny replied. "I'm not exactly having a great day."

"Until I arrived?" he asked innocently.

"Let's see what kind of tennis player you are," she said, making a halfhearted attempt at a joke.

When they arrived at the courts, the afternoon sun beginning to lower behind the three-story brick high school, Claire and Rick were already playing. Rick was clowning around as usual, trying to return the ball from behind his back. Claire looked a lot like a flamingo, Jenny thought, her long legs exposed under white tennis shorts.

As Jenny and Cal pulled open the gate and entered the court, Claire and Rick stopped their game. Jenny apologized for being late.

"I'm sure you have a good excuse," Rick said, flashing her his goofy smile, sweat pouring down his broad forehead.

"Yeah. Somebody put a dead tarantula in my bag," Jenny said bitterly.

"Aw, come on. You can do better than that," Rick joked.

Jenny didn't laugh. She gave him a dirty look instead. Then she introduced Cal to them.

"I'm going to Harrison in the fall," Cal said, pointing to the high school with his racquet.

"Lucky duck," Rick said sarcastically.

"Can we play?" Claire urged, looking at her watch. "It's getting late."

They divided up, Claire and Rick on one side, Jenny and Cal on the other. They warmed up a bit and then began to play. It became quickly obvious to Jenny that, as with the skating, Cal was not quite the beginner he claimed to be. In fact, he was a skilled player.

What a phony, Jenny thought, watching him serve. Why does he always have to act as if he's never tried something before?

"Out! That was out!" Rick called, sounding angry for some reason.

"It was in, I think," Cal said quietly.

"No way! It was out!" Rick insisted heatedly.

Cal sighed, shrugged, and served again. Rick hit it back hard, nearly taking Cal's head off.

"Hey — " Cal cried, ducking back, surprised.

"Come on — show us something," Rick challenged him, gripping the racquet in his beefy hands.

"Rick — chill out. What's your problem?" Claire asked.

Rick ignored her. He continued to challenge Cal.

I've never seen Rick like this, Jenny thought. He's usually so relaxed, so easy-natured.

"That was out!" Rick called, red-faced.

It was clearly in, Jenny thought. What is Rick trying to prove?

As the game continued, the two boys seemed to forget the girls were there. This isn't a game, thought Jenny. It's a personal battle of some kind.

Shouting and cursing, the boys batted the ball back and forth. Both of them seemed to grow angrier and angrier.

"Double fault!" Rick cried.

"What?" Cal screamed and angrily tossed his racquet at the net. He came running toward Rick, fury in his eyes. Rick moved forward, dropping his racquet, prepared for a fight.

But Cal stopped at the net. He was breathing hard, glaring at Rick.

Rick stopped, too, and bent to pick up his racquet.

"That's it," Claire declared. "I quit."

Rick turned around, looking startled to find her still there. "Hey — sorry," he called to her, raising his T-shirt to mop his sweaty forehead.

"What's with you today, Rick? What's all the yelling and carrying on?" Claire asked him, clearly disgusted.

"It works for McEnroe," Rick declared, his good humor beginning to return.

"I've got to get home anyway," Jenny said, feeling confused about what had just happened.

"Nice meeting you guys," Cal said, bending over to pick up the racquet he had thrown.

Claire walked over to Jenny and bent down to whisper in her ear. "I think Rick put on his little show for *you*."

"Huh? What do you mean?" Jenny asked, bewildered.

"I think Rick was showing off for *you*. Why else would he be acting so weird?"

"I don't know. Maybe his tennis shorts are too tight," Jenny cracked.

As usual, Claire didn't laugh at Jenny's joke. Her face, flushed from the exertion of the game, remained thoughtful.

Jenny suddenly noticed that Rick was staring at her, as if seeing her for the first time. His face was bright red. His black hair was matted down from all the sweat.

"See you," Jenny said, giving him a little wave.

"Yeah," he called. "Come to the shoe store sometime. I'll show you how to work a shoehorn."

Jenny laughed even though it was a stupid joke. She waited for Cal to catch up with her. They crossed the street and headed toward her house. "Some game," Jenny said.

Cal apologized. "He kept egging me on, challenging me," he explained. "I guess I just got carried away."

"He's usually not like that," Jenny said, taking his arm.

"Neither am I," Cal replied. "Hey — I forgot to tell you," he said, stopping and turning to her. "I got a job. At Mulligan's. You know — the ice-cream store in the mall. For the rest of the summer."

"That's great!" Jenny exclaimed. "Can you get me a discount on a double-scoop cone?"

"Sure," Cal said, smiling. "You'll have to come meet me there sometime. I can probably get you sprinkles on it, even. If you're good."

"Oh, I'm very good," Jenny said playfully.

They were at the bus stop. "This is where I get

off," Cal said. "I've got to get home. Here comes the bus." He reached into his pocket for change.

"See you soon," Jenny said. "Save me some mint chocolate chip. That's my favorite."

She watched him climb onto the bus, still thinking about the angry competition of the tennis match. Cal seems so nice, she thought, watching the bus pull away. But he sure lost his temper at Rick.

She wondered if she was seeing the real Cal when they were together, or whether he put on an act for her.

She hoped she was seeing the real Cal.

Then carrying both racquets, still replaying the events of the day in her troubled mind, she walked slowly home.

"I don't believe it!" Mrs. Wexner cried, holding her hands up to her face to show her surprise.

Sitting at the kitchen counter the next morning, Jenny had just told her about the dead tarantula.

"That's impossible," Mrs. Wexner insisted, gulping down the last drop of coffee in her cup, nearly dropping the cup as she tried to replace it on its saucer. "Why would Eli do that, Jenny?"

"As a joke, I think," Jenny replied. "A practical joke."

"But Eli cares about those awful tarantulas as much as — as anything he owns," Mrs. Wexner said. "I just can't imagine him killing one of them in order to play a stupid joke on you."

She glanced nervously at her watch, stood up,

and carried the cup and saucer to the sink. Her toast lay on its plate, uneaten. "I'm late, but we've got to get to the bottom of this."

She motioned for Jenny to follow her, and the two of them hurried up the stairs to Eli's room. They found him tapping away at his computer keyboard even though he hadn't had breakfast yet.

"Eli — " his mother called cautiously.

He typed a while longer, then turned around. He looked at his mother, then at Jenny. His face didn't reveal much emotion at all, just mild annoyance at having been interrupted.

"Eli, did you play a joke on Jenny?" his mother demanded accusingly.

"Huh?" His narrow face filled with innocent surprise.

"Did you put a dead tarantula in Jenny's bag?" Mrs. Wexner asked, getting right to the point.

"My tarantulas aren't dead!" Eli exclaimed, looking over at the cage. The idea seemed to upset him immediately.

Mrs. Wexner gave Jenny a puzzled glance.

Jenny stared at Eli, trying to see through this innocent act he was putting on.

"Eli, no one's angry at you," Mrs. Wexner said softly. "We just want to know if you played a joke on Jenny."

He shook his head no.

Mrs. Wexner is afraid of her own son, Jenny thought.

"You didn't give her a tarantula?"

"They're *my* tarantulas!" he insisted. "I'm not giving them to anybody."

"But, Eli, I found a tarantula in my bag yesterday," Jenny said, speaking softly as his mother had done. "You're the only person I know who has tarantulas. So — "

"Take a look," Eli said, jumping up and walking over to the glass cage.

Jenny and Mrs. Wexner quickly joined him there.

"Look," Eli said, pointing. "One, two, three. They're all here."

Jenny counted them, too. Sure enough, all three tarantulas were inside, two of them crawling around, one of them motionless, pressed up against one of the corners.

"I'm sorry, Eli," Jenny said quickly, feeling very confused and embarrassed.

"You shouldn't say I did bad things when I didn't," Eli said angrily, crossing his thin arms over his chest.

"Jenny said she was sorry," Mrs. Wexner said, coming quickly to Jenny's defense. But she gave Jenny a suspicious look.

"I'm really sorry," Jenny said, leaning down and putting her hands on Eli's slender shoulders.

He immediately pulled away from her. "Go away," he said sullenly. He turned and started to walk away. And then suddenly, he uttered a loud wail and burst into tears.

Jenny froze in surprise. She'd never seen him cry before.

His mother rushed to comfort him, throwing her arms around him and pulling him into a tight hug.

But Eli continued to wail, a high-pitched wail like a baby might make, his eyes shut tight, large tears rolling down his cheeks.

"Eli, I'm sorry. I'm sorry!" Jenny called. But he was crying too loudly to hear her.

With a loud burst of anger, he pulled out of his mother's hug and flung himself face down on the bed, crying into the bed sheet, slapping his fists in a fury against the mattress.

"We'd better leave him alone for a while," Mrs. Wexner whispered. Horrified, feeling terribly shaken and guilty, Jenny followed her back downstairs.

Why on earth is Eli carrying on like this? Jenny asked herself, her mind racing from thought to thought. Is he *that* hurt that I accused him unjustly? Or is he making a big scene to cover up his guilt?

I *didn't* imagine the tarantula, Jenny thought. I *didn't* imagine it!

"I'm afraid you've gotten off to a bad start with Eli this morning," Mrs. Wexner said, shaking her head as she glanced at her watch. "But he'll come around. Just let him cry it out. Then be really nice to him."

"I feel so bad — " Jenny started.

"Oh, I'm really late. Got to run." Mrs. Wexner grabbed up her car keys from the low table by the door.

"I guess someone else played the joke on me," Jenny said uncertainly.

Who? Who would do that? Who else would get a dead tarantula to stuff in her bag? Who could get into her bag without her knowing it?

Mrs. Wexner didn't seem to have heard what Jenny said. "Good luck with Eli. Just be careful with him. Once he stops crying, be extra nice to him," she instructed, and disappeared out the back door, heading to the garage.

She didn't care at all, Jenny thought bitterly, hearing the car grind for a few seconds and then start up. She doesn't care about anything but keeping Eli calm.

The little monster had to be the one who put the tarantula in the bag. He *had* to. And then he replaced the dead one with a new one.

But I'll never prove that.

And what's the point?

One more story to tell Dr. Schindler. One more thing for him to suggest maybe I made up.

She slumped onto the bench in front of the kitchen counter and chewed off a bit of Mrs. Wexner's cold toast. It tasted like cardboard. She could barely swallow it.

Dr. Schindler isn't helping me at all, she decided. I feel more uncertain about things, about myself, now than ever. I don't feel any more confident. I don't feel as if I'm getting anywhere.

And what if I really did imagine those phone

calls? What if I really am cracking up?

She shook her head as if trying to shake away the glum thoughts. Then she walked to the stairwell and listened.

Silence. The crying seemed to have stopped.

She listened for a while longer. Then, satisfied that he wasn't crying, shouted up, "Eli! What do you want for breakfast?"

No reply.

"Eli?"

"Go away!" he screamed, still sounding angry and out of control.

She started up the stairs. "Eli — you've got to have breakfast."

"Go away! Go away! Go away! I don't want to see you! I *don't*!" he shrieked.

She was halfway up the stairs when she heard a loud crash. Eli screamed. Then she heard another crash that sounded like something heavy falling.

"Eli — what was that?"

Silence.

She flew up the rest of the stairs, two at a time.

"Eli — are you okay?"

Silence.

Into his room, a scene of disarray.

The bedclothes had been stripped off the mattress and tossed in a tangle on the floor. The desk chair lay on its side in the middle of the room. Books and papers and art supplies were scattered everywhere.

And sprawled on his back on the carpet lay Eli, his eyes frozen in a glassy stare, his head tilted at an odd angle, his mouth hanging slack and unmoving, one arm bent underneath him, a puddle of dark blood under his head.

Chapter 13

"Eli?"

This isn't happening, she thought.

The room began to spin. She grabbed the side of the door for support.

The puddle of blood seemed to grow brighter until it glowed. She looked away. Then looked back. It had returned to its wine-dark color.

"Eli?"

She ran to him, knelt down on her knees, lifted his head in her hands. He stared up at her with glazed, unseeing eyes.

"What have you done? How did this happen?"

"Beats me," he said, and started to giggle.

"What?" Jenny screamed, dropping his head in shock.

He laughed and sat up.

"Eli — " Jenny's heart was in her throat. She felt as if she were going to be sick.

He picked up the puddle of blood. It was fake. Some sort of plastic. He tossed it at her, laughing

107

hysterically, slapping his hand on the carpet.

"*Why did you do this?*" Jenny shrieked, anger rising up from her chest, feeling herself losing control. "How could you scare me like that?"

"Easy," he said. He stopped laughing, but couldn't keep a wide, pleased grin off his face.

"Didn't you know how much that would scare me?"

"Yes."

That grin — Jenny wanted to wipe it off his face. She wanted to hit him. She wanted to make him cry, make him *bleed*.

She *hated* him!

No.

Get control, Jenny. Calm down. Just calm down. He's a little boy. He's only ten years old. And he's very confused.

Calm. Calm. Calm.

No matter how many times she repeated the word to herself, it just wouldn't work.

"Hey — you said you wanted me to play a joke on you," Eli said, tugging her sleeve.

"I did not, Eli. That's not what I said at all."

His grin faded, replaced by a look of disappointment. "You said I played a joke on you before, but you were wrong. So I decided to play a joke on you now."

"But that was a *horrible* joke. You scared me to death!"

He laughed, still holding her T-shirt sleeve. "That means it was a *good* joke."

"Don't ever do that again," Jenny scolded. "To anyone."

He picked up the plastic sheet of blood and rolled it around in his hands. "I'm hungry," he said. "I want breakfast."

He isn't sorry at all, she realized. In fact, he's the happiest I've ever seen him.

"Come on downstairs," she said, finally feeling strong enough to climb to her feet. "Let's see what we can make you for breakfast."

He led the way out of the room, skipping gleefully to the hallway. Jenny stopped at the doorway and glanced back at the tarantula cage. All three of them were scrabbling all over each other in what appeared to be a concerted attempt to get out.

The phone rang at four-thirty, interrupting their Monopoly game. "Don't answer it," Eli said, shuffling through his property cards.

"I have to," Jenny told him, climbing up from the living room floor. "It might be your mom and dad. You know, they're not coming home till very late tonight."

"You're staying with me?" he asked, a worried expression on his face.

"Of course. I wouldn't leave you here alone," Jenny said, hurrying toward the phone, which had already rung three times.

Eli had acted insecure all day, clinging to her, practically attaching himself to her, never letting her out of his sight. He's such a strange kid, Jenny thought. Sometimes he can be so cold and aloof, so grown-up in a way. And today he's been acting like a little baby.

She picked up the phone receiver and heard loud breathing on the other end. A cold shudder of dread rolled down her back.

"Hello?"

"Hello, Jenny?"

She didn't recognize the voice immediately.

"Jenny, it's me."

She felt her throat catch. Her fear, she realized, was always right below the surface, ready to take over, ready to grab hold of her at the slightest provocation.

"It's me — Chuck," the voice said.

She felt her anger push away the fear. "Chuck — what do *you* want?" she asked coldly. Eli looked up at her from across the room, startled by the harshness of her voice.

"Jenny, I — "

"You hurt me, Chuck," she interrupted, the painful memory flooding over her, feeding her anger.

"I — listen, I know. I just need to talk to you." His voice trembled with emotion.

She realized she didn't care.

"Chuck — have you been following me around?" she demanded.

He didn't reply.

"Well? Have you? Have you been spying on me?"

Still no reply.

"You really hurt me, Chuck."

"I know. I just — "

"Stop calling me." She was shouting now, probably upsetting Eli, but she didn't care. She couldn't help herself. "I mean it. Stop spying on me, and stop calling me."

"Now, wait just a minute, Jenny — "

"Don't ever call me again." She slammed down the receiver.

Keeping her back to Eli, she stood in front of the phone, trying to calm down, taking deep breaths, waiting for her heartbeat to return to normal.

I shouldn't have yelled like that, she thought. I don't want to alarm Eli. He's been so strange and insecure all day.

She turned around to face him, prepared for his questions, prepared to try to deal with his confusion and anxiety.

To Jenny's surprise, he had a smile on his face. "You landed on Park Place," he said. "You have to pay me."

The rest of the day went smoothly. Jenny put a frozen pizza in the oven for dinner. Eli ate two slices hungrily, even though he complained that it was too tomatoey. Then he ran up to his room to work on his computer.

Jenny sat on the sofa by the living room window, staring out at the front yard as the sky faded from pink to gray, and then to black.

The darkness seemed to renew her fears, bring them out from their hiding place, make them dance across her mind. Staring out the window, she heard the frightening whispers again.

"*I'm back.*"

"*Company's coming.*"

Who could it be?

Who was trying to terrorize her? Who knew those words, those exact words that held such terror for her?

Chuck knew them. Chuck knew the whole story.

A few other friends knew the story, too.

And, of course, Mr. Hagen knew them.

Crazy Mr. Hagen. *Dead* Mr. Hagen.

"*Jenny, I'm back.*"

She stood up, determined to find something to do, to drive these thoughts away, to force the fear back to its hiding place, when she heard the knock on the front door.

A hard, forceful knock that caused her to cry out in alarm.

The knock repeated, louder.

She stepped into the front hallway.

"Who's there?" she asked, unable to keep her voice from trembling.

Chapter 14

Jenny pulled open the front door.

"Hi, Jenny."

She stared at Rick and Claire as if she didn't recognize them. "Hey — what are you two doing here?"

Rick stepped past her into the hallway. "Some greeting," he muttered.

Claire held out a package of M&M's and dumped some in Jenny's hand. "Your mom told us you were here," she said, following Rick into the house.

"Hey — not bad," Rick said, admiring the living room.

"How's it going?" Claire asked, around a mouthful of candy.

"Not bad," Jenny said uncertainly. "We had a bad incident this morning, but — "

"Where's the little spaz?" Rick asked, looking around the living room.

"Don't call him that, whatever you do," Jenny warned. She suddenly realized that she had become as frightened of Eli as his parents were.

"I love little spazs," Rick said, grinning his goofy grin. "I was a little spaz myself once."

"*Now* what are you?" Jenny couldn't help but crack.

Rick looked hurt. He plopped down heavily on the couch.

"Hope you don't mind us coming here," Claire said, bending down to scratch a scrape on her knee just under the hem of her tan shorts. "We thought you might like some company."

"Well, I'm not sure it's such a good idea," Jenny said, feeling more than a little apprehensive.

Her eyes went up to the top of the stairs where Eli suddenly appeared. "Who are they?" Eli demanded, sounding suspicious.

"There he is!" Rick said, laughing for some reason. "Hi, guy. I'm Rick."

Eli ignored him. "What are they doing here?" he asked Jenny.

"These are my friends," Jenny said. "Come down and meet them."

"I don't want to," Eli said, shaking his head.

"Well, then stay upstairs and meet them," Jenny told him. "This is Claire and this is Rick."

"But what are they *doing* here?" Eli repeated, whining.

"They came to visit me. You're being very rude, Eli," Jenny said.

"You like to play basketball?" Rick asked, grinning up toward Eli.

"Want some candy?" Claire held up the envelope of M&M's.

Eli continued to ignore them. "I don't want them here," he told Jenny.

"Eli — that's not nice. These are my friends," Jenny said impatiently.

"I don't care. I don't want them here."

"We're only going to stay a short time," Claire said, looking at Jenny.

"Tough little dude," Rick muttered, pushing the sofa cushion as if testing it out.

"It's my house," Eli said.

"Aren't my friends welcome in your house?" Jenny asked, sounding more shrill than she had intended.

Eli didn't reply.

"Sure you don't want some M&M's?" Claire offered again.

"Maybe," Eli said, softening just a bit.

"I'll bring 'em up to you," Claire said, smiling at him and starting up the stairs. "Can I see your room? Jenny told me you've got a lot of great stuff in your room."

Eli shrugged. "Yeah. I guess."

Claire was definitely winning him over, Jenny saw.

"You into Ninja Turtles?" Rick called up to Eli.

Eli ignored him and, as Claire joined him on the upstairs landing, held out his hand for her to pour candy into. Then he and Claire disappeared into Eli's room.

"I think the spaz is hard of hearing or something," Rick griped.

"I think he was ignoring you," Jenny said, laughing. She sat down on the other end of the couch and tucked her legs beneath her.

"Kids love me," Rick said, brushing back his dark, curly hair. "They're usually all over me."

"He's not a regular kid," Jenny said.

"If I ever talked to company like that, my parents would really come down on me," Rick said.

"I don't think Eli gets punished too much," Jenny replied, whispering in case Eli was listening. "I don't think he'd react too well to being punished. He's very high-strung. He has an IQ of 800 or something."

"Weird," Rick said. Then suddenly he reached over and took Jenny's hand. "Hey — your hand is cold."

"Is it? I hadn't noticed," Jenny said uneasily.

He rubbed her hand as if trying to warm it. Then he slid over to Jenny on the couch and put his arm around her shoulders, pulling her close.

Jenny was so surprised, she didn't react at first.

Rick had never acted the least bit interested in her — except as a friend. What was this about?

His big arm felt heavy on her narrow shoulders. He leaned forward, moving his face toward hers, about to kiss her.

"Rick — whoa!" She tried to pull away, but he had her pinned down. "Hey — stop."

He immediately pulled his arm away. She jumped to her feet.

"What's going on?" she asked, more puzzled than upset.

He shrugged. "Just kidding around," he said. But his face was bright red, and his hurt expression revealed that he was more serious than he was letting on.

"Rick, you and Claire and I have been friends — " Jenny started.

"Forget it," he snapped, his face still crimson. "Just forget it." He seemed really angry.

Jenny didn't want to hurt him. She didn't know what to say. She felt very confused.

Rick scowled and stared out the window.

Jenny started to say something but was interrupted by shouting from upstairs. "What was that?" she asked.

Claire and Eli seemed to be having some sort of an argument.

"No, you can't!" Eli was screaming. "I *said* no!"

"What's the little spaz carrying on about now?" Rick asked, still avoiding Jenny's glance.

Jenny started to the front stairs. She was halfway across the living room when she heard Claire scream.

Then she heard the *thud-thud-thud* of someone toppling down the steep staircase.

"Oh, no! Eli!" Jenny cried.

But it wasn't Eli.

She reached the stairs in time to see Claire hit the bottom step, then drop onto the floor.

"Claire — are you all right?"

Claire didn't reply. She lay on her back, her eyes opened wide, her face still locked in an expression of terror, her neck bent at an odd, unnatural angle.

"Claire? Claire?" Jenny cried.

Rick was right behind her now. "How did she fall?"

"I don't know," Jenny replied, bending over her unmoving friend. She grabbed Claire's shoulder. "Claire — are you okay? Can you hear me?"

Claire didn't move.

"She's unconscious," Rick said, on his knees next to Jenny. "She's knocked out."

"Claire?" Jenny looked for some kind of a response, *any* kind of response.

Then, suddenly remembering Eli, she turned her glance to the top of the stairs. Eli stood on the landing, leaning against the banister, staring down at them. Jenny gasped when she saw that he was grinning, his eyes twinkling merrily under the yellow hall light.

Chapter 15

"He was standing at the top of the stairs, just grinning down at us. Enjoying it. I think he was really enjoying it, Dr. Schindler," Jenny said, sitting up rigidly on the couch. She was much too worked up to lie back.

"Sometimes people laugh or smile when they're nervous or scared," Dr. Schindler said thoughtfully, sucking on the eraser end of a yellow pencil.

"What do you mean?" Jenny asked.

"I mean, Eli may have been very frightened. He may not have realized that he was grinning. It's very normal for people to have inappropriate facial expressions when they're under stress."

"Well, Eli didn't look too stressed out to me," Jenny insisted. "There was Claire lying at the bottom of the stairs, totally unconscious. And there was Eli grinning down at us like it was some kind of joke. Or one of those slasher movies that he loves so much."

"Go on with the story," Dr. Schindler said, putting down the pencil. "What happened next? Did you call an ambulance?"

"Yes. I called 911. They sent an ambulance and some paramedics. It didn't take long for them to get there. I don't know how long, exactly. But Claire woke up before they arrived."

"She was okay?" the psychiatrist asked.

"Yeah. Pretty much," Jenny told him, fiddling with the sleeve of her T-shirt, pulling it nervously up and down. "Her head hurt. She hit it pretty hard on the way down. And she pulled a muscle in her shoulder. That's what they said at the hospital. But aside from that, Claire was okay. I mean, she felt pretty shaky for a while. But she was okay."

"And how did the accident happen?" Dr. Schindler asked.

"I'm not so sure it *was* an accident," Jenny said, raising her eyes to see the doctor's reaction.

He waited for her to continue, his face as expressionless as always.

"I mean, Eli said it was an accident. He said Claire ran out of his room and just slipped and fell down the stairs," Jenny explained, still picturing the gleeful grin on Eli's face. "But when I talked to Claire after she got home from the hospital, Claire told me she thought she was pushed."

"By Eli?" the doctor asked, leaning back in his chair.

"Yes. She wasn't really sure. It happened so fast.

But Claire thinks that Eli pushed her down the stairs."

"She wasn't sure?"

"No." Jenny shook her head. "But if Eli didn't push her, why was he grinning like that?"

"What do you think?" Dr. Schindler asked.

"I don't know."

"Do you think Eli pushed your friend, Jenny?"

"I don't know. I don't know what to think, Dr. Schindler."

"Do you think this ten-year-old would deliberately try to hurt someone, maybe even kill someone?"

"I . . . I don't know."

"Well . . . do you think Eli is *evil*?"

Jenny thought hard about it. "Maybe . . ." she said.

"How is your friend doing?" Mr. Wexner asked, struggling to tie his necktie.

"She's fine," Jenny said, dropping her backpack on the hallway floor. She was wearing faded powder-blue denim cutoffs and a sleeveless green T-shirt. "It's sweltering out there," she said, trying to change the subject.

Mr. Wexner turned away from the hall mirror to look at her. "We didn't know you had planned to have some friends over." He tried to say it lightly, but it was obvious he was scolding her.

"I didn't plan it. They surprised me," Jenny said

defensively. And then she added, "It won't happen again."

Especially since your son is a demented *killer*, she thought.

She knew she was exaggerating, but she couldn't help it.

She wondered if she'd ever be able to look at Eli again without thinking of the way he grinned down at poor, unconscious Claire.

"Eli was pretty upset about what happened," Mr. Wexner said, giving up on the knot and starting all over again. "He didn't say anything, but — "

At that moment, Eli came charging into the hallway. He ran into Jenny, nearly knocking her over, and threw his arms around her in a tight, affectionate hug.

"Eli — " his father started, surprised.

Eli continued to hug Jenny, pressing his head into her waist. Jenny patted his head tenderly. Her terrible thoughts about him started to melt away.

He's just a little boy, she thought.

He's just a troubled, spoiled little boy.

How could I have thought he was some kind of evil monster?

"I want to give you a kiss," he said.

As Mr. Wexner looked on in obvious surprise, Jenny leaned down and Eli gave her a noisy kiss on the cheek. Then he let go of her and, without saying another word, ran up the stairs to his room.

"Eli has really taken to Jenny," Mr. Wexner said

to his wife as she entered the hallway from the back of the house.

"Really?" She couldn't hide her surprise.

"I've never seen him be so affectionate with anyone," Mr. Wexner said. And then he quickly added, "Outside the family, I mean."

"He's very sweet," Jenny said, still feeling Eli's warm lips on her cheek.

"He is!?" Mrs. Wexner exclaimed, staring at Jenny. "Eli?"

Mr. Wexner laughed. "You should've seen him. He's obviously nuts about her. What a display!"

A thought crossed Jenny's mind: Maybe Eli was being so affectionate because he felt guilty about the other night.

Jenny scolded herself for being so suspicious. Maybe he just *likes* you, she told herself.

The Wexners left a few minutes later, still talking about how affectionate Eli had been toward Jenny. Jenny went to the bottom of the stairs and, standing on the spot where Claire had lain so still, so lifeless, called up to Eli. "What are you doing up there?"

"Nothing," came the reply from somewhere deep in Eli's room.

"Want to play a game or watch a tape or something?" Jenny asked.

"No," was Eli's curt reply. "I'm busy."

Probably pounding away on his computer, Jenny thought. She took a book out of her backpack and plopped down on the couch to read. Outside the living room window, a light drizzle fell. The sky was darker than usual, the blackness interrupted by gray-yellow clouds lined up eerily in straight rows. The rain, tossed by gusting winds, pattered in waves against the window, receded, then pattered noisily again.

Jenny read for about half an hour, listening to the rain against the glass. She was reading *Wuthering Heights*, one of her summer reading books. Such a romantic book, she thought. Wish I lived back then. Wish I could go walking on the moors with a handsome young man dressed for the hunt. . . .

Suddenly realizing she hadn't heard a sound from Eli's room, she closed the book and headed toward the stairs to investigate. The phone rang just as she passed it.

Startled, she picked it up before the first ring had ended. "Hello?"

"*Hi, Babes.*" The whispered voice. "*Are you all alone?*"

"Hey — " Jenny cried angrily.

"*Company's coming, Babes. Company's coming.*"

Her heart pounding, Jenny slammed down the receiver. She pressed her head against the wall and shut her eyes tight.

Who was it?

Who was doing this to her?

People didn't come back from the dead. They just didn't.

She forced herself not to panic, remembering

that she was on her way to Eli's room.

What was Eli doing up there, anyway? Why was he so quiet?

She tried to shut the hoarse, whispering voice out of her mind, to think about Eli instead of the frightening phone call.

She reached the top of the stairs, took a few steps toward Eli's room — and then stopped.

And listened.

A voice. She heard a voice coming from the room. But not Eli's voice.

Someone was in Eli's room, talking very quickly in a low whisper.

A hoarse whisper.

Jenny leaned back hard against the wall to keep from falling.

Everything started to spin. The floor tilted, then appeared to float up toward her.

Jenny had to force herself to breathe. Her fear tightened her throat, pinned her against the wall.

It was him!

The whisperer.

He was there — in Eli's room!

Chapter 16

What has he done to Eli?

Is Eli okay?

Holding her breath, her back still against the wall, Jenny began to edge slowly toward Eli's room.

She could hear the hoarse, whispered voice but couldn't make out the words.

He's on the phone, she realized.

He's whispering to someone else.

She stopped just before the open doorway. Pale white light poured out into the hall. She could hear the whispered voice speaking haltingly now into the phone.

Who is it?

How did he get into the house?

Where is Eli?

She had to find out.

With a burst of courage, Jenny grabbed the door molding, leaned forward, and peered into the room.

Eli sat at his counter, his back to her.

He had the receiver of his homemade phone to his ear. He was whispering hoarsely into the receiver, disguising his voice.

"Eli!" Jenny screamed.

He dropped the receiver onto the phone and spun around to face her. His face filled with surprise at first, then reddened with guilt.

"Eli!" she repeated, looking frantically around the room to make sure no one else was there with him.

No. Eli was alone.

"You scared me!" he cried, his lower lip trembling.

"What were you doing?" Jenny demanded.

He didn't reply. "You scared me," he repeated, quieter this time, avoiding her accusing stare.

"Answer my question, Eli. What were you doing?"

"Nothing," he said defensively. "Playing."

"Eli — I saw you talking on the phone."

"So what? It's *my* phone."

"Who were you talking to?" Jenny demanded, walking up to him, standing over him, forcing him to look at her. "Who?"

"Why are you so angry?" he asked, his voice growing tiny and frightened. "I was just playing jokes."

"Jokes?"

"Yeah. You know. Calling people. Saying funny things."

"You whispered things?" He looked away. She repeated the question. There was no way she was going to let him off the hook.

"I just said funny things. That's all." He shrugged. His tone turned impatient, irritable.

"Who did you call?" Jenny asked, putting her hands firmly on the narrow shoulders of his T-shirt.

"Kids from school," he told her. "Just kids I know."

"Did you call *me*?" Jenny asked.

He stared into her eyes as if trying to decide which answer she wanted to hear.

"Did you?" she repeated, squeezing his shoulders. "Eli, did you call me?"

"Yes," he said, his face a blank.

Jenny took a deep breath and let it out.

Was this possible? The frightening calls? Was it really possible that this innocent-looking ten-year-old was responsible?

"Don't you remember?" Eli asked. "I called you late at night. You were the first person I called on my phone."

"Huh?" Jenny realized she had read too much into his answer. Eli wasn't confessing after all. "What about tonight? Eli, did you call me a few minutes ago?"

He stared at her. "I told you. I just called friends."

She stared back at him, but she couldn't tell if he was telling the truth or not. Suddenly he reached forward and hugged her again, wrapping his spindly arms around her waist. He held onto her for a long time. Jenny couldn't see his expression. She put a hand tenderly on his shoulder, wondering if she had misjudged him or not.

After a while, he let go and sat back in his desk chair. He looked up at her, his face bathed eerily in yellow light from his desk lamp, making him look pale, ghostlike, a strange smile on his face. "Jenny, tell me about your other baby-sitting job," he said.

The rain had stopped when she reached the parking lot at the Walker Mall. A steady stream of cars, pale beams of light from their headlights steaming in the wet night air, flowed out of the lot as Jenny pulled in.

For a moment she pictured the parking lot as a vast, dark ocean, and here she was struggling to move against the tide.

She eased the car past the closing stores, her tires splashing through the deep puddles on both sides of the lane. She slowed to a crawl as she passed by Mulligan's, the ice-cream store. The last customers were walking out with cones. She couldn't see Cal inside. The store lights dimmed. She pushed down on the gas and headed toward the spot where they had arranged to meet.

What was so familiar about those large, green, clothing bins? she wondered.

She parked the car, cut the headlights, and rolled

down the window. Such a steamy night. The air felt thick and soupy. Perspiring, Jenny opened the door and climbed out.

A few dark cars dotted the enormous lot. Employees' cars, most likely. Jenny suddenly felt chilled despite the steamy heat of the night.

Why did this all seem so familiar?

Lights shifted and flickered across the vast, dark ocean, making it look to Jenny like waves bobbing and tumbling as far as she could see. More stores darkened. The stream of cars exiting the parking lot slowed to a trickle.

Jenny paced between her car and the green clothing bins. She felt nervous, fluttery, and couldn't figure out why.

I should have met Cal at the ice-cream store, she thought, her eyes surveying the empty lot. I don't know why he wanted me to meet him in this remote corner.

She squeezed the sides of her hair. Wet from the humid air. I must look a mess, she thought.

Where *is* Cal?

He probably had to clean up after the store closed.

I could use an ice-cream cone right now, she thought. Or maybe a sundae.

"Cal — where are you?" she called aloud.

More store lights darkened. The waves of the parking lot seemed to toss as the light changed.

Footsteps.

Jenny heard the splash of shoes through the puddles, the thud of feet hurrying across the wet pavement.

Someone is running toward me.

And in that instant, the dream returned. She suddenly remembered it all. . . . Waiting in this corner of the parking lot. Pacing back and forth under the yellow street lamp. Peering out through the darkness. Waiting, waiting.

And then the hand reaching out from the clothing bin. The odorous, decayed form pulling itself out, slogging toward her. Mr. Hagen, back from the dead, back to get his revenge on her.

It all came back to her.

She could see it so vividly and feel the fear. Fresh fear.

Fresh, paralyzing fear.

Here she was again, in this very same parking lot, in this very same spot.

In the very same dream.

And the footsteps grew louder. Faster.

Wake up, Jenny. He's coming after you.

Wake up. Wake up. Wake up.

Only this time it wasn't a dream.

This time she couldn't wake up from it.

This time it was real.

She uttered a desperate cry and started to run.

Chapter 17

Cold rainwater splashed over her sneakers as she ran. The footsteps, steady, rhythmic, continued to come toward her.

Which way? Which way? she asked herself, her panic causing her to stop just beyond her car.

Which way out of this dream?

The parking lot seemed to roll and tumble. Wave after wave, and once again, she was struggling against the tide.

Which way? Which way?

Wake up, Jenny. Please — wake up safe and sound in your bed at home.

No.

She had to run. She had to get away.

The footsteps wouldn't go away.

This was real. Real danger.

Fresh fear.

I'll run toward the stores, she thought. I'll run toward the light.

So why wouldn't her legs cooperate?

Impulsively she spun around to face her pursuer.

He stepped slowly out of the shadows.

"Dr. Schindler!" she cried. Panic and surprise tightened her voice to a shrill whistle.

His face filled with surprise. He was balancing a bulging, brown-paper grocery bag awkwardly against one shoulder. He had a dark stain on one leg of his chinos. His white sneakers were wet and muddy.

"Jenny?"

"Dr. Schindler. You — you frightened me," Jenny stammered.

What is he doing here? she asked herself. Why does he look so nervous?

He glanced quickly around. "I never can find my car in these big parking lots," he said. "Are you . . . waiting for someone?"

"Yes. A friend. Here he comes now."

Dr. Schindler turned to see Cal crossing the lot, both hands stuffed in his pockets. He shifted the grocery bag onto his other shoulder. "Hey — there's my car. Way down there. I see it now." A smile crossed his face as he pointed.

Jenny waved to Cal.

I really am cracking up, she thought.

Why did I run from Dr. Schindler? Why didn't I wait to see who was approaching?

It was the dream, she told herself.

For a moment, I was back in the dream.

You're crazy. Crazy. Crazy. The word repeated in her mind, drowning out what Dr. Schindler was saying to her.

"What?" she asked.

"I said good night." He still looked very nervous and uncomfortable. "I'm sorry if I frightened you."

"Good night," Jenny said, looking over Dr. Schindler's shoulder at Cal, who started to jog toward her.

Struggling with the grocery bag, Dr. Schindler hurried off to his car. "Who was that?" Cal asked, running up to Jenny.

"My shrink," Jenny said and took Cal's arm.

"Huh? What's he doing here?"

"Buying groceries, I guess," Jenny said, watching Dr. Schindler's dark Saab glide away toward the exit.

"You okay?" Cal was studying her face intently.

"He scared me, that's all. I mean . . . I don't know," Jenny said, feeling frightened again, feeling not in control, feeling as if she might burst into tears or start screaming.

Crazy. Crazy. Crazy.

"I had a dream, and it sort of came true," she told Cal, realizing that it wasn't much of an explanation.

"Want to go somewhere and talk?" Cal asked tenderly, slipping his arm around her shoulder. He smelled of ice cream. Chocolate. Strawberry.

"Yes." She decided she wanted to tell him everything, everything that was happening to her, the

134

threats, the cold, whispered threats from the man she had sent to the grave. "Yes," she said. "I — I'm in trouble, kind of."

He held the car door open for her. "I'm a good listener," he said softly. "I've been in trouble, too."

She turned and studied his face, shadowy in the dim yellow light. The scar on his chin suddenly seemed deep and dangerous. "What kind of trouble?" she asked.

He shrugged in reply and closed her car door.

They drove to a Wendy's on the south side, empty except for three sullen teenagers in a front booth and an old man sleeping over a cup of coffee. Jenny led Cal to a table against the back wall, and over french fries and Cokes, told him the story from the beginning, starting with the night she went to work baby-sitting for the Hagens.

She told him about the attacks on baby-sitters all over town. She told him about the frightening telephone threats she began to receive.

She told him how it was Mr. Hagen who made the threats, who attacked the baby-sitters.

She told him about the terrifying night when Mr. Hagen forced her to the rock quarry outside town where he had planned to kill her and had ended up dead himself, plunging over the side to the rocks below.

She told him about the new phone calls, about the whispered voice so filled with menace. The whispered threat: *"Jenny, I'm back. Jenny, company's coming."*

She told him about Chuck, about Chuck's violent temper, about how Chuck was the only other person who knew Mr. Hagen's exact words to her.

And she told him about Eli, what a strange boy he was, and how she had caught him making furtive, whispered phone calls.

She started to tell Cal about finding the dead tarantula in her bag when she realized who it was who was trying to terrify her.

It came to Jenny in a flash.

She stopped in midsentence, her mouth dropped open, her dark eyes growing wide.

She had solved the mystery.

Chapter 18

"Jenny — what's wrong?"

Jenny didn't reply. She was thinking too hard about her sudden inspiration.

"Jenny?" Cal reached across the table and took her hand. "Earth calling Jenny."

"Oh. Sorry." She smiled at him, but she still wasn't ready to talk.

Her mind felt super-charged, as if she could feel electricity coursing through her head, through her entire body.

Suddenly, everything — or almost everything — made sense.

She knew she was right. She knew she had just solved the mystery. But knowing the answer didn't solve the problem.

And knowing who was doing it didn't tell her why.

"Whoa. Jenny — you're a million miles away," Cal complained, still holding her hand.

"You've got ketchup on your arm," she said, pointing.

They both laughed. The laughter helped to bring her back to Cal. She pulled a napkin out of the dispenser and helped wipe the sticky ketchup off his arm.

"I just solved the mystery," she told him. "While I was talking to you."

"I *told* you I'm a great listener," he said.

"I know who's been calling me. I know who's been trying to frighten me."

He balled up the ketchup-stained napkin and tossed it into a glass ashtray. "Jenny — who?"

"Dr. Schindler."

Cal didn't react at all, just stared at her, expressionless.

"Didn't you hear me? It's Dr. Schindler," she repeated, pounding the table for emphasis.

Cal narrowed his blue eyes thoughtfully. But he still didn't say anything.

"You don't believe me — do you?" Jenny accused.

"Why Dr. Schindler?" he asked, finally finding his voice.

"I know it's him," Jenny said. "It has to be him."

"Why?" Cal repeated. He watched over her shoulder as the three teenagers got up and left, bumping each other as they made their way out the glass door.

"He's the only one who knows the whole story. Don't you see?" Jenny asked. There was a plea in her voice. Please believe me, she was saying to Cal.

"Yeah. But what does that prove?" Cal asked, staring hard at her as if trying to penetrate her mind, invade her thoughts.

"I've told him everything," Jenny said excitedly. "Every detail. Every word Mr. Hagen said to me. Dr. Schindler is the only other person besides Chuck who knows everything."

"So what makes you think it isn't Chuck?" Cal asked, rolling the plastic salt and pepper shakers in his hands.

"Chuck is angry at me because I broke up with him," Jenny explained. "But he isn't really a bad guy. He was with me all through that terrible time. He helped me a lot. He knows what a nightmare it was. He would never try to scare me about it. He would never pretend to be Mr. Hagen. I know Chuck. Even with his bad temper, he'd never do that to me. He just wouldn't."

Cal thought about it for a while, fiddling with the salt and pepper. "So we're back to my original question: Why Dr. Schindler?"

"I don't really know why," Jenny said thoughtfully. "I mean, I don't know why he's doing it to me. I just know he's the only one it could be. I've gone over the story about Mr. Hagen with him again and again. Dr. Schindler knows every detail, every dream I've had about it, every thought I've had, every fear."

"But, Jenny — "

"And he looked so nervous at the mall parking

lot tonight, so uncomfortable," Jenny continued, not giving Cal a chance to break her train of thought. "What was he doing there, Cal? His car wasn't even near mine. What was he doing there?"

Cal started to say something, but Jenny answered for him.

"It wasn't a coincidence. He was following me. I'm sure of it. He wanted to scare me. He knew about my dream that took place there. He knew. You know, I'm remembering more things about him now," Jenny said, thinking hard.

"Like what?" Cal asked, rubbing the scar on his chin.

"Like how he always asks me where I'm going and where I'm going to be."

"What do you mean, Jenny?"

"He always wants to know if I'll be baby-sitting at the Wexners or not. He's always so curious about where I'll be after my sessions with him. And why is that?"

"Because he's really interested in you?" Cal suggested.

"No. He's only interested in his clock. In finishing on time and getting on to the next session. He isn't really interested in me. It's just a job to him. But he asks me those questions about where I'm going to be because he wants to know where to call. He wants to know where I'll be so he can frighten me. It's so obvious!"

She looked at Cal, eager for him to agree with her. But his face was still filled with doubt.

"Why, Jenny?" he asked. "You have to answer that question. Why would Dr. Schindler do that to you? Why would he try to frighten you?"

"Maybe he's crazy," Jenny suggested. She flung up her arms in frustration. "I don't know! Maybe it's a new kind of shock therapy!"

Cal laughed. He stopped when he saw the irritated look on Jenny's face. "There's no motive," he said. "Dr. Schindler has no motive."

"But if it isn't Dr. Schindler, it has to be Mr. Hagen," Jenny said, fear tightening her features. "If it isn't Dr. Schindler, that means Mr. Hagen really is back. That means I'm being pursued by a dead man, a zombie, some kind of monster. I really don't want to believe that, Cal. I really don't."

"Maybe it's the little boy," Cal suggested quietly.

"No," Jenny insisted. "It's Dr. Schindler. I know it is. I should have known the second I saw that look on his face in the parking lot. I should've known." She grabbed Cal's hand. "I'm going to prove it, Cal."

His eyes narrowed as he studied her face, still trying to read her thoughts. "How? How are you going to prove it?"

"I'm going to set a trap for him," Jenny said. "You've got to help me, Cal. You've got to. Even if you don't believe me, you've got to help me."

Chapter 19

"The doctor is running a little late this morning,"
Miss Gurney said, looking up from her typewriter.

"That's unusual," Jenny replied, glancing around
the empty waiting room. Her eyes stopped at the
tropical fish tank built into the wall. The fish all
seemed to be darting wildly up and down.

They're as nervous as I am today, Jenny thought.

"I just fed them," Miss Gurney said, following
Jenny's glance. "I like your hair, dear. Did you do
something new to it?"

"No. Just washed it this morning," Jenny said
absently, fascinated by the frenzied fish. She walked
up to the tank to get a better look.

"Such a lovely color," Miss Gurney continued. "I
always wanted dark brown hair like yours. Mine
was always such a mousey color. So washed-out."

The inner door opened, and Dr. Schindler poked
his head out, looking all around the waiting room.
"Good morning, Jenny. Admiring the fish?"

"Look at them. They're going crazy!" Jenny exclaimed.

"Crazy isn't a word we use in this office," Dr. Schindler said, pursing his lips.

Jenny realized he had just made a joke, so she forced a brief laugh.

"Shall we begin?" He dropped some files onto Miss Gurney's desk, then motioned for Jenny to follow him into the office.

Even the fish know something strange is going on here, Jenny thought. She took a seat on the leather couch.

Dr. Schindler slid into his chair and pulled it up to the desk. He looks tired, Jenny thought. He looks as if he were trying to look super-alert and energetic to hide the fact that he is tired.

You're hiding something, Jenny thought.

You're hiding something. But I'm going to get it out into the open.

I'm going to end all this so I can go on with my life.

She felt a sudden tremor of fear.

Here I am, closed up in this room with the man who has been threatening me.

He's a monster. A Jekyll and Hyde.

But not for much longer.

"You seem very pensive today," he said, leaning forward, elbows on the desk, propping his chin in his hands, concentrating all of his attention on her.

Jenny didn't know how to reply to that, so she waited for him to go on.

143

"What would you like to talk about today?" he asked.

"Well . . ." Jenny started, taking a deep breath, clasping her hands together tightly in her lap. "I have this idea."

"Idea?"

"Yeah. About how to stop my nightmares. You know. How to get this all behind me."

"I'd like to hear your idea," he said quietly, staring into her eyes.

"Well, it's just a feeling I have."

"A feeling? Can you describe it?"

"Well," Jenny said, pretending to be working it out in her mind even though she had rehearsed this carefully. "These nightmares. These fears. I just have the feeling I'm never going to leave them behind me unless I face them head-on."

She stopped and looked to see how he reacted.

"Go on," he said, his face a blank.

"Well," she continued, wondering what he was really thinking, "to cut right to the chase, my idea is to go back to the rock quarry."

His eyes blinked wide in surprise. Then he quickly resumed his blank expression.

"To go back to the quarry. At night. To face this thing down. To show myself that there's nothing there. That it's just a pile of rocks. That there's nothing in that rock quarry that's going to come after me. I know it sounds crazy. . . ."

He cleared his throat. "As I said, we don't use that word around here."

"I just have the feeling that if I face it again, face it one last time, I can put the whole dreadful experience behind me," Jenny said. "And then maybe the nightmares will stop, and the strange phone calls, the strange thoughts that flash through my mind. Everything will go away."

She watched him carefully to see if he'd react when she mentioned the phone calls. But he remained stone-faced.

"I can see you've given this a great deal of thought," he said finally, seeming to choose his words carefully. "And I think your idea is an interesting one, and one we should discuss." He cleared his throat again. "But I feel that it is my obligation to warn you, Jenny, that there is no quick solution to your problems. No easy answer. We should try everything we can. And mainly, we should continue to talk. But you've got to realize that this could be a very long process. Years, even. You've suffered quite a trauma, let's not forget. The kind of trauma that most people never experience in a lifetime. With time, I think you will find your life, your thoughts, your subconscious thoughts, all will return to what we could call normal."

She stared at him, trying to figure out what was going on in his mind while those smooth, professional words were coming out.

Are you thinking about your next whispered phone call, Dr. Schindler? Are you thinking about what threat you're going to whisper next time?

Jenny wondered if he had other patients he terrorized, or if she was the only one.

Why me? she wondered. Why me?

"So are you recommending that I *not* go back to the quarry?" she asked.

He picked up his desk clock and rolled it between his hands. "Not necessarily," he said. "It's hard to say. It might be beneficial in some ways. Or it might serve to deepen your anxieties."

"I'm going to do it," Jenny said decisively, sitting up straight. "I've made up my mind, Dr. Schindler. I just *know* it's going to help me."

"Well, if you feel so strongly . . ." he started.

"I'm going there tonight!" Jenny declared.

Dr. Schindler switched off his tape recorder.

"Good luck," he said.

Something about the way he said it gave Jenny the chills.

Chapter 20

"Jenny, I'm back."

Jenny, lost in thought, felt a jolt as she heard those words. She spun around to see Eli smiling at her.

"What did you say?" she asked.

"I said I'm back," Eli repeated impatiently. "I went out to get the mail. I put it on the kitchen table."

"Oh." Jenny realized she was breathing hard.

"Are you okay?" Eli asked.

"Yes. I'm fine. I was just thinking about something else," Jenny said, giving his hair a playful tug.

After her session with Dr. Schindler, she had been distracted all afternoon. She had barely paid any attention at all to Eli. And when Rick had called to apologize for acting like a jerk, she had cut him off quickly without really meaning to, leaving him thinking that she was still mad at him.

All she could think about was the rock quarry. She kept picturing it in her mind, seeing it at night the way she had seen it the first time. The flat, hard, barren ground leading up to the quarry. The enormous deep, dark pit. The sheer drop. The sharp rocks far down below, jutting up in the darkness.

Thinking about going there brought back all of the terror of that dreadful night last fall. But Jenny's mind was made up. She knew she had to do it. She had to make the nightmares stop.

She had to end the constant fear, all of the fear.

She had to expose Dr. Schindler.

Then she had to get on with her life. . . .

She was thinking about her dream for the millionth time — seeing Mr. Hagen, his dead flesh rotting away, climbing up from the quarry pit, coming after her — when Mrs. Wexner returned home.

"Oh. Hi," Jenny said, jumping up from the couch, shaking her head hard as if trying to shake her thoughts away.

"How was Eli today?" Mrs. Wexner asked, stepping out of her high heels, rubbing her feet through her sheer stockings.

"Fine," Jenny said. She realized she hadn't paid much attention to Eli. I'll make it up to him on Saturday, she thought.

Eli appeared in the living room doorway, chocolate stains around his mouth. "Eli, what have you been eating? It's almost dinnertime," Mrs. Wexner scolded.

"Nothing," Eli replied, unaware that the chocolate gave him away.

"Well, say good-bye to Jenny. She's leaving."

Without warning, Eli came rushing up to Jenny and gave her an enthusiastic hug. She hugged him back briefly, then started toward the door, but he wouldn't let go.

He clung tightly to her, pressing his head against her waist.

It's as if he knows something is going to happen, Jenny thought. It's as if he senses that I'm about to do something dangerous.

That he might never see me again.

She scolded herself for letting her imagination run away with her. Eli doesn't sense anything, she told herself. He's just trying to make it difficult for me to leave.

"I'll see you on Saturday," she told him, gently prying him off her. She made her way quickly to the front door and hurried out without looking back.

I *hope* I see you on Saturday, she thought.

I hope I'm still alive on Saturday.

As she walked home, a red sun lowering in a cloudless, darkening sky, she could see the quarry opening up in front of her, see the endlessly deep pit, the deadly rocks awaiting below.

She started to run along the curb and, lost in her dark, frightening thoughts, nearly ran past her house before she realized where she was.

She forced herself to be cheerful at dinner, making up funny anecdotes about Eli to tell her mother. She wondered if her mother could tell that she was putting on an act.

Cal picked her up in his little car a few minutes after seven-thirty. He seemed nervous and serious, his eyes flat and lusterless, without their usual sparkle.

"Why don't we just go to a movie?" he suggested, only half-kidding.

"After tonight, we can go to the movies every night," Jenny said, squeezing his arm.

They were out of town, driving through farmland now, the dark fields interrupted by occasional silos and low farmhouses.

"What do you think is going to happen?" Cal asked, his eyes on the road, both hands gripping the top of the wheel tightly.

The question took Jenny by surprise.

She had spent so much time thinking about the past, about what had happened at the quarry, about Mr. Hagen, about her dreams, her nightmares, that she hadn't given much thought to what would happen when she actually returned to the quarry.

"I don't know," she said edgily. "I guess I'll look around and remember everything."

"You already remember everything," Cal interrupted.

"You're not being helpful," Jenny said sharply. "Don't give me a hard time."

He quickly apologized, his eyes on the road.

"I know this seems crazy to you, Cal, but you haven't lived inside my skin for the past six months. You haven't had my nightmares."

The farms gave way to barren flatlands. Theirs

was the only car on the narrow road.

"Dr. Schindler will be there," Jenny continued. "I know he will. He'll try to frighten me. But he won't be counting on you being there."

"What am I supposed to do?" Cal asked, trying to sound calm and businesslike but unable to keep the worry from his voice.

"Just be there," Jenny said. "I think that'll be enough. Once Dr. Schindler sees that he's been found out, he'll give up. He'll run."

"What if he wants to fight or something?" Cal demanded.

"He's a shrink. He won't fight," Jenny said. "He'll be afraid of you, Cal. You look tough. He's probably never been in an actual fight in his life."

"Are you telling me the truth?" Cal asked, following the road as it curved through the dark, flat countryside.

"Of course I am," Jenny told him. "Don't worry. He won't fight. When he sees you, he'll run."

"Maybe he won't show up," Cal said.

"Right," Jenny said sarcastically. "Maybe Mr. Hagen will show up instead. Maybe my nightmare will come true and Mr. Hagen will leap up out of the quarry with his skin falling off and his skull showing, and he'll grab us both and take us back to his grave with him."

Cal didn't reply.

"I'm sorry," Jenny said quickly. "Don't pay any attention to me. I'm just nervous."

"Don't worry," Cal said softly. His face, caught

in the bright headlights of an oncoming car, looked hard as if set for trouble. She had never seen that expression before. "I'll be right here," he said through gritted teeth.

For some reason, those words, meant to comfort her, gave her a sudden chill.

Cal hit the brakes hard, startling her, and turned off the road. The small car bounced onto a bumpy dirt road.

"Cal — what are you doing?" Jenny cried.

"I almost missed the turnoff," he said. "It isn't very clearly marked. Guess they don't expect many visitors at night."

"We're here," Jenny said, thinking aloud.

"Afraid?" he asked.

She wanted to answer, but her reply caught in her throat.

Chapter 21

Cal cut the engine and switched off the headlights. The world went completely black for a moment. Then Jenny began to make out dark shapes and shades of black and gray.

She pushed open the car door, took a deep breath of the hot, humid air, and stepped out onto the hard rock ground. Cal took her hand as they walked toward the quarry edge.

"It's different," Jenny said, whispering, squeezing his hand tightly. Her hand was ice-cold. His felt warm and dry. "Those piles of gravel," she whispered, pointing to the tall, dark mountain shapes around them, "they weren't here last fall."

"Guess they've been working here," Cal whispered back.

"Strange," Jenny whispered as they walked closer to the edge. "This place was deserted for years."

"How do you feel? Are you okay?" Cal asked. He put an arm heavily around her shoulder.

Straight ahead, about twenty yards away, lay the enormous pit. Jenny couldn't see it. She could just make out where the ground stopped and gave way to total blackness.

"I'm frightened, but I'm okay," Jenny whispered.

"Can we leave now?" Cal asked.

She couldn't tell if he was serious or not. "Go hide over there," she said, pointing to the nearest mound of gravel.

"Maybe I should just stay here with you," he insisted, his arm around her tightly.

"No," she said. "I want to stand here alone. I want to face this alone. And — "

She stopped.

They both saw the flash of light in the trees. Car headlights.

They could hear a car bumping along the dirt road.

The lights went out. Then the car sounds stopped. Far down the road.

"Dr. Schindler. I knew it," Jenny whispered excitedly. Her heart pounded in her chest. She gave Cal a soft shove. "Quick. Hide. Behind that gravel."

"But, Jenny — " He started to protest, but changed his mind and jogged off to the gravel pile. "I'll be right here," he called back in a loud whisper. He disappeared behind the dark mound of stones.

Jenny stood alone, breathing hard, her eyes surveying the dark mounds around the quarry. Behind her lay the open pit, black and silent.

No ghosts here tonight, she thought, reassuring herself.

No one back from the grave.

Just me. And Cal. And a visitor. A living, human visitor.

She stood still as a statue. Watching. Listening.

She could hear the crunch of footsteps approaching, hurrying over the hard ground.

I hear you, Dr. Schindler, she thought.

I hear you. I'm waiting for you.

I'm ready for you. . . .

Her senses seemed to be heightened by her fear. She could smell the rocks. She could hear each approaching footstep. She felt as if she could see the *air.*

I'm ready. I'm ready. . . .

And then suddenly, the dark figure loomed in front of her.

"Jenny, I'm here." The hoarse, whispered voice.

Closer, closer. Until Jenny could see her pursuer perfectly.

"You!" Jenny cried in astonishment. "What are *you* doing here?!"

Chapter 22

"Jenny, I'm here."

"But — why?" Jenny cried, taking a step back as the figure moved closer.

"Company's coming."

"I don't believe it!" Jenny cried. "Why *you*?"

Miss Gurney took another step toward Jenny. Her hair, usually tied tightly behind her head, dropped wildly about her face. She wore baggy black slacks and a black blouse, long-sleeved despite the heat.

"Why?" Jenny cried, still stunned at the identity of her pursuer. "Why have you been doing this to me?"

"You can't have him," Miss Gurney said in her hoarse voice. She stopped advancing on Jenny and put her hands on her wide hips.

"What? I don't understand," Jenny exclaimed.

"You can't have him," Miss Gurney repeated. "You can't have Dr. Schindler."

"But — but — I don't — "

"You have boyfriends. Lots of boyfriends," Miss Gurney continued, spitting out her words scornfully. "You have everything, don't you! The pretty hair. The nice clothes. And the boyfriends. I know. I know everything about you, Jenny. I listen to the tapes. They tell me everything."

"Miss Gurney, I really don't know why — "

"Shut up!" the woman screamed, moving forward in a rage. "Shut up! Shut up! Shut up! You can't have him! I've seen the doctor with his hand on your shoulder. I've seen how he talks to you. He hardly says a word to me."

"I'm just a patient!" Jenny screamed.

"I was a patient, too!" Miss Gurney shouted back. "But now he ignores me. Day after day, he ignores me. While you get all the attention. He spends hours listening to your tapes. He spends hours talking with you. Why should you have everything? Why can't I have *anything*?"

"Please — calm down," Jenny pleaded. "Let's talk, okay?"

I've got to keep her talking, Jenny thought. Maybe I can make her see that this is all crazy. Crazy!

"Calm down," she said. "Let's have a nice, quiet talk about Dr. Schindler. Just you and me."

"I *won't* calm down!" Miss Gurney screamed, backing Jenny closer to the quarry edge. "Why should I calm down? The doctor doesn't even look at me anymore. But he looks at you. At your pretty, clean hair. At your pretty, dark eyes. Oh, he looks

157

at you, all right. With your nice clothes. And all of your nightmares. All those nightmares to talk about. To talk about with *my* doctor for hours and hours. All those nightmares I listened to on your tapes."

Miss Gurney paused to take a breath. "Well, guess what, Jenny? Guess what? *I'm* your nightmare now. *I'm* your nightmare. And there's no Dr. Schindler to tell it to. There's just you and me, dear."

"I don't understand. Let's just talk," Jenny begged as Miss Gurney drew closer. "You made those frightening phone calls? You put the dead tarantula in my bag while I was in seeing the doctor?"

"I just wanted you to notice me," Miss Gurney said, lowering her voice ominously. "I just wanted you to know that I knew what you were up to. That I wouldn't let you get away with it. *And I won't!* You can't have him! You can't have him!"

"What are you going to do?" Jenny asked, backing away from the steadily approaching woman.

"You're going to die like that poor Mr. Hagen died," Miss Gurney said.

Without further warning, she rushed at Jenny, her arms outstretched, ready to push Jenny over the quarry edge.

"No!" Jenny screamed. "Cal! Help!"

She saw Cal leap out from behind the mound of gravel, running at full speed.

Startled by the unexpected sound of someone

behind her, Miss Gurney turned. "What?" she cried. "Who's there?"

With a loud groan, Cal leaped at her, intent on tackling her, bringing her to the ground.

But Miss Gurney dived to the ground just as he leaped.

Cal sailed over the startled woman.

And as Jenny watched in horror and disbelief, Cal plunged over the edge, headfirst into the quarry.

Chapter 23

He's gone, Jenny thought.

Cal is gone.

I've killed him. Just as I killed Mr. Hagen.

Killed my own friend.

Jenny saw Miss Gurney climbing slowly to her feet, a pleased smile on her face, her hair flying wildly about her head.

And then Jenny saw the hand reach up over the quarry side.

My dream, she thought in horror. My dream is coming true.

A second hand appeared on the edge of the pit. And then two arms.

It's Mr. Hagen, Jenny thought. He really has come back.

She stood, frozen to the spot, paralyzed as in the dream. And she waited to see the decaying flesh, the empty eye socket, the grinning, evil face of the dead man.

But the face that appeared at the edge of the pit wasn't Mr. Hagen's. It was Cal's.

Soaking wet, Cal pulled himself up onto the ground.

The quarry — it's been filled with water! Jenny realized.

She had screamed so loudly when Cal plunged over the side that she didn't hear the splash.

"Cal — are you okay?"

She started toward him, but Miss Gurney grabbed her around the waist.

"Let go!" Jenny cried, struggling to free herself.

"You can't have him! You can't!" Miss Gurney shrieked, squeezing Jenny's waist, trying to wrestle her over the edge.

"Let go!" Jenny repeated.

The big woman was surprisingly strong.

"You can't have him! You can't have him!"

She gave Jenny a hard push, then toppled on top of her.

Jenny felt the ground disappear, saw the dark water loom up.

Both of them plunged into the cold, still quarry water.

Down, down. Miss Gurney held tightly, wouldn't let go.

Jenny flailed her arms and legs. She tried to kick the big woman away with her knees.

But Miss Gurney held Jenny's waist in an ever-tightening grip.

So cold. So heavy.

So dark in this water.

Dark as death.

They floated to the surface, their heads popping above the water.

Both gulped in mouthfuls of air.

"Let go!" Jenny managed to cry.

She pushed Miss Gurney hard, and the woman lost her grip on Jenny for a moment.

Sputtering, kicking, Jenny tried to swim to the edge.

But Miss Gurney grabbed her arm, pulled her back, then pushed her head under the water.

She's too strong, Jenny thought.

Her rage makes her strong.

She kicked at the woman and pulled with all her strength.

But Miss Gurney had a tight grip on Jenny's head, pushing down with both hands now.

Dark. Then darker.

Dark as death.

Cold as death.

Jenny flailed frantically but couldn't free herself.

Her lungs felt about to burst.

Miss Gurney pushed her down, down, holding her head below the surface.

I'm going to drown, Jenny realized.

I'm starting to drown.

I can't hold my breath any longer, Jenny thought, as everything turned bright red.

Chapter 24

Up, up.

She was floating up. Up through the water. Still red.

Everything was still red.

Flashing on and off. Red then black. Red then black.

Where was Miss Gurney?

Gone.

Lost in the red. Everything so red.

Have I drowned?

No. Jenny realized she was breathing.

Someone was holding onto her. Pulling her up.

Cal.

"Cal — it's you?"

He was pulling her out of the water. She felt so heavy. So tired and so heavy. Like a rock.

Like a rock from the quarry.

"Cal — why is everything so red?"

He pulled her up and held her close. The world started to come back into focus.

There were cars all around. And men. Flashing red then black. Red then black.

Jenny realized that the flashing red lights were on top of cars. Police cars.

Several police officers were trying to fish Miss Gurney out of the water. She splashed and screamed. She wasn't cooperating. She was refusing to come out.

"Cal, we're okay," Jenny said, resting her head against his soaked shirt.

"Yeah. We're okay," Cal said quietly. "I got her off you just in time."

"You're okay!" a man's voice cried.

He stepped out of the shadows, into the blinking red light.

"Dr. Schindler!" Jenny cried, holding tightly to Cal. "How? I mean — why?"

"I brought the police," Dr. Schindler said. "You're okay? You're both okay?"

"Just wet," Jenny said. "But how did you know?"

"I couldn't find your tapes this evening. They were missing. Completely gone. Then I figured out what was going on," Dr. Schindler said. "I should have figured it out when you first told me about the phone calls. I just didn't think."

"Miss Gurney — " Jenny said pointing toward the water, where the frantic woman was still screaming at the police, still splashing in the water.

"She had violent, jealous episodes before," Dr. Schindler said. "That's what I treated her for. She was doing reasonably well, I thought. She had worked for me for three years without incident. But when I saw that she had taken your tapes, I knew she had to be the one who was frightening you. And I knew that she would come here tonight after listening to today's tape. I'm just so glad you're okay."

Apologizing again for not figuring it out sooner, Dr. Schindler hurried down to the quarry edge to try to help persuade Miss Gurney out of the water.

"You two can leave," a policeman said quietly. "Get into some dry clothes. We'll get a statement from you later."

Jenny thanked the policeman.

Cal, his arm around Jenny's shoulder, gently led her toward the car. "Had enough of the quarry?" he asked.

"Yes," she nodded, shivering. "I don't think I'll ever need to see this horrid place again."

"Good," he said, holding open the car door for her. "Does this mean we can go to the movies instead?"

She stood facing him, one hand on the car door, one hand on the soggy front of his shirt. "Yes. From now on. The movies," she said. "What would you like to see?"

"Well . . ." — his laughing eyes sparkled in the

GREEN WATCH by Anthony Masters

BATTLE FOR THE BADGERS
Tim's been sent to stay with his weird Uncle Seb and his two kids, Flower and Brian, who run Green Watch – an environmental pressure group. At first Tim thinks they're a bunch of cranks – but soon he finds himself battling to save badgers from extermination . . .

SAD SONG OF THE WHALE
Tim leaps at the chance to join Green Watch on an anti-whaling expedition. But soon, he and the other members of Green Watch, find themselves shipwrecked and fighting for their lives . . .

DOLPHIN'S REVENGE
The members of Green Watch are convinced that Sam Jefferson is mistreating his dolphins – but how can they prove it? Not only that, but they must save Loner, a wild dolphin, from captivity . . .

MONSTERS ON THE BEACH
The Green Watch team is called to investigate a suspected radiation leak. Teddy McCormack claims to have seen mutated crabs and sea-plants, but there's no proof, and Green Watch don't know whether he's crazy or there's been a cover-up . . .

GORILLA MOUNTAIN
Tim, Brian and Flower fly to Africa to meet the Bests, who are protecting gorillas from poachers. But they are ambushed and Alison Best is kidnapped. It is up to them to rescue her *and* save the gorillas . . .

SPIRIT OF THE CONDOR
Green Watch has gone to California on a surfing holiday – but not for long! Someone is trying to kill the Californian Condor, the bird cherished by an Indian tribe – the Daiku – without which the tribe will die. Green Watch must struggle to save both the Condor and the Daiku . . .

MYSTERY THRILLERS

Introducing a new series of hard-hitting action-packed thrillers for young adults.

THE SONG OF THE DEAD by Anthony Masters

For the first time in years "the song of the dead" is heard around Whitstable. Is it really the cries of dead sailors? Or is it something more sinister? Barney Hampton is determined to get to the bottom of the mystery . . .

THE FERRYMAN'S SON by Ian Strachan

Rob is convinced that Drewe and Miles are up to no good. Where do they go on their night cruises? And why does Kimberley go with them? When Kimberley disappears Rob finds himself embroiled in a web of deadly intrigue . . .

TREASURE OF GREY MANOR by Terry Deary

When Jamie Williams and Trish Grey join forces for a school history project, they unearth much more than they bargain for! The diary of the long-dead Marie Grey hints at the existence of hidden treasure. But Jamie and Trish aren't the only ones interested in the treasure – and some people don't mind playing dirty . . .

THE FOGGIEST by Dave Belbin

As Rachel and Matt Gunn move into their new home, a strange fog descends over the country. Then Rachel and Matt's father disappears from his job at the weather station, and they discover the sinister truth behind the fog . . .

BLUE MURDER by Jay Kelso
One foggy night Mack McBride is walking along the pier when he hears a scream and a splash. Convinced that a murder has been committed he decides to investigate and finds himself in more trouble than he ever dreamed of . . .

DEAD MAN'S SECRET by Linda Allen
After Annabel's Uncle Nick is killed in a rock-climbing accident, she becomes caught up in a nerve-wracking chain of events. Helped by her friends Simon and Julie, she discovers Uncle Nick was involved in some very unscrupulous activities . . .

CROSSFIRE by Peter Beere
After running away from Southern Ireland Maggie finds herself roaming the streets of London destitute and alone. To make matters worse, her step-father is an important member of the IRA - if he doesn't find her before his enemies do, she might just find herself caught up in the crossfire . . .

THE THIRD DRAGON by Garry Kilworth
Following the massacre at Tiananmen Square Xu flees to Hong Kong, where he is befriended by John Tenniel, and his two friends Peter and Jenny. They hide him in a hillside cave, but soon find themselves swept up in a hazardous adventure that could have deadly results . . .

VANISHING POINT by Anthony Masters
In a strange dream, Danny sees his father's train vanishing into a tunnel, never to be seen again. When Danny's father really does disappear, Danny and his friend Laura are drawn into a criminal world, far more deadly than they could ever have imagined . . .